GODWIN HARPINSHIELD'S CALLING

A familiar pressure started to build at the back of Godwin's mind. He was being Called, and there was only one safe place to be when that happened. Home. Godwin scribbled a signature on the bill, having forgotten by what name they knew him here—not that it mattered, for none of his bills was ever presented for payment—and rushed back to the car.

Time was growing short. The pressure in his head sent bright shooting lights across his field of vision. Miraculously, there was a space in front of the house. He parked and scrambled out without bothering to lock up. If someone stole his car, he could always buy another. Half-blind with pain, Godwin rushed upstairs and, not sparing time to turn the room on, spent the last moments of awareness desperately trying to reach a decision about his Reward.

Inspiration struck him—he didn't have to choose! *They* knew Rewards he could never think of. Had Irma requested her Sirian plants? Had Hermann known about the alien's amazing powers? When had Hugo & Diana experienced free fall?

Thankful, convinced, Godwin Harpinshield surrendered.

And was Used.

Also by John Brunner
Published by Ballantine Books:

Players at the Game of People

by

John Brunner

A Del Rey Book

BALLANTINE BOOKS • NEW YORK

THE air was literally filthy. Godwin Harpinshield passed his tongue across his lips and it reported to his teeth and palate grit: dust from the daytime air raid which had not yet settled. And now, again, already, sirens were caterwauling under a darkling summer sky.

There was a slight ache in his right leg, but it was not unbearable. Rather, it was almost pleasant, indicative of a healing wound. He had on too many clothes for such warm weather; his feet sweated in tightly laced black shoes, while on his head was a cap with a stiff peak. He was, to be precise, wearing an RAF officer's uniform with—he glanced at the cuffs—flight lieutenant's badges of rank. On his left breast were pilot's wings. His left palm and fingers were sticky, holding a pair of obligatory brown leather gloves. Smoke made his eyes and nose tingle, but a breeze was disturbing the still air as the sun went down.

Not that it could be seen from here, for he stood between double ranks of tenement houses that had known better days, faced partly with brick, partly with blue and yellow tile. Their windows were taped with brown adhesive paper and their doorways were labyrinthed with high walls of khaki sandbags. Here and there bites had been crunched out of their upper stories, as though a crazy aerial dog had clamped enormous jaws on what it mistook for food, then spat out disgusting rubble on the roadway. Prompted by the sirens, people could be seen turning lights off and drawing thick blackout curtains. None of the streetlamps was on.

Picking its way among piles of débris, here came a

lumbering double-decker bus with its headlights masked. He stood at a bus stop, a temporary post on a street too narrow for public transport to use under normal circumstances, even though not a single car or van was to be seen parked along it. The reason for the detour was made plain by signs at the street's two ends: DANGER—BOMB DAMAGE—NO RIGHT/NO LEFT TURN. Respectively.

A resigned voice said, "Oh, damn. Just when a Number Eight finally turns up."

There were others waiting at the bus stop: a tired elderly couple, two teenage girls with teeth like discolored tombstones.

Overhead a night fighter left a faint straight vapor trail from west to east. A searchlight beam sprang up and swiveled in great jerky arcs. At one point in its traverse it touched the silvery side of a barrage balloon, creating a fragment of artificial moon. Behind the sirens a drone began, the sound of several hundred bombers.

One of the girls said, "They're coming back, then," as flatly as though making a comment about the weather.

Almost in the same second there were soft crumping explosions: the reports of ack-ack shells far to the east, from ground batteries in Kent and along the Medway. The bus halted, but not to pick up passengers, only to discharge those it had. The driver stopped his engine and scrambled to the ground, cursing. Not yet middle-aged, he looked old. His flesh was pulpy, testimony to years of a diet based on bread and marge and bacon.

Even as the passengers descended, grousing but not objecting, half a dozen boys and elderly men appeared from nearby doorways, donning tin hats marked fore and aft with the letters ARP, standing for "air raid precautions." The same acronym could be seen on numerous posters giving advice about what to do when the Luftwaffe struck at London. In an area where most people could scarcely read their own names, all those lines of close black print were clearly fruitless. The people milled about like frightened ants as they spilled into the roadway.

The ARP wardens did their amateur best, shouting through cupped hands that in the next street, out of sight but there all the same, a basement had been designated as an official shelter. But moving that way meant heading east, toward and not away from the noise of gunfire and by now probably the first salvos of bombs, and they were overwhelmed as the other occupants of the buildings came flooding forth. At first a trickle, then a spate of families with small children, led by women because almost all active men had already gone to war, rushed headlong toward the more credible sanctuary of a tube station a few hundred yards to the west.

Knowing when they were beaten, the wardens tried at least to keep the fugitives orderly. But the children, roused from bed and hastened into the street in nightclothes or tattered underwear, were frightened. They cried. Some of them screamed. Urgency threatened to turn into panic. The wardens shouted, but could not make the crowd obey. There was too much noise; there was the wail of sirens like banshees riding an invisible storm; there were ever more explosions, some of which by now must be from bombs dropped on Port of London, because the racket of enemy aircraft was almost deafening—well over a hundred in this wave alone, each with a pair of thousand-horsepower engines; also there were shrill police whistles and the bells of fire engines and ambulances and the grinding *slump* as structures of brick and tile and concrete were laid low by the devastating onslaught.

Abruptly a vast redness lit the eastern sky. A heartbeat afterward there followed a puff of hot sound. Something very burnable had been hit: oil, wax, maybe even munitions. The people's cries and fears redoubled as they arrived at the tube station and realized how narrow the entry was, how steep the stairs beyond.

At least the station staff were having the grace not to insist on the legal penny-halfpenny fare from every adult, though they were in duty bound to do so. Some duties, their humanity advised, must take precedence over what was officially laid down. These people, Godwin thought with a glow of pride, could never staff extermination camps . . .

But mere goodwill was not enough. Here was a crowd on the point of becoming a leaderless mob. Suppose a child tripped and was trampled to death!

Godwin took mental stock of his condition. The pain in his leg indicated one potential weakness, for it came from a bullet wound. But it was nearly healed. In contrast, the fact that he wore this of all uniforms would stand in good stead. Much publicity had made the world familiar with such a shade of gray-blue, and with RAF wings . . . even though he was already being looked at resentfully by some, as though his presence— that of a warrior armed against the foe—might conjure down a doom on this street rather than another.

Alternatively: *what's he doing here instead of flying his plane and killing Jerries?*

Then the thrill of a right decision reached ran through his spare frame.

A few paces ahead of him was a woman wearing a gray coat over a nightdress, clutching a baby and trying to keep track of three little girls, all blond, all thin, all peaky from the undernourishment which had beset this nation during the Depression and which careful rationing of food had not yet rectified. Aged perhaps three, five, and seven, they gazed about them in dumb and wide-eyed wonder, as though fancying they were still in dreamland, where parents' orders did not have to be attended to.

The ground shook. Flakes of brick and mortar shivered from the façades of nearby buildings. Also the eastern sky was aflame as more and more incendiary bombs planted the seeds of inferno across the city.

Already the people converging on the station entrance were elbowing each other and shouting insults. In a minute there might be a fight. Wildfire was among the ancientest of terror-symbols; what to take as a symbol of calm?

That wizened three-year-old: she would do perfectly. With a stride and a wince and a stride Godwin was beside her, sweeping her into his arms as though he were her father.

"Come on now, you *men*!" he barked in his most parade-ground tone. There were some men helping to jam the stairs, and they were old enough to recall the other war. "Women and children first! Here, make sure these little girls are safe!" And he disposed of his own load—not unthankfully, for her hair and her very clothes were greasy to his touch—to the tallest man within reach on a lower step, and turned to pick up her sister.

It worked. The panic halted. They handed the children over their heads at first—and some giggled and squealed, but at least they weren't screaming in terror—and the dense press of people lessened as those below dispersed along the platforms, soothing the youngsters. In a moment or two it was possible for women to follow, the men standing aside to let them through. Backs straightened. There were smiles, especially from the wardens overjoyed at this helpful intrusion on the part of a member of the officer class, this renewed proof that it was always safe to rely on Squire.

Later, of course, nightly descents into the bowels of London would become commonplace, but now it was weird and incredible that one should lie on hard, cold platforms among neighbors who until today were strangers. The Germans had only just shifted their attention from airfields to cities; the name "Battle of Britain" was freshly coined. It was a beautiful summer and should never have been despoiled by those clouds of smoke, those pillars of rising dust.

Certain policemen were hovering, who had orders from Whitehall to refuse admission to the tubes during a raid. They were embarrassed, and shuffled their feet, and made no move to comply with their instructions.

As soon as they had an excuse to move off, like the shrill of ambulance bells, they seized it gratefully and disappeared.

"Thanks very much, sir," said a warden from under the shadowing brim of his helmet. "We needed somebody to take charge." He moved slightly to let latecomers go by; now there was a steady, controlled, regular flow descending the stairs, and someone was trying to start a singsong with "Roll Out the Barrel."

"Last night," he added, "my old woman fell down and got 'er arm broke. Wouldn't 'ave been too much worse off if Jerry'd got 'er," he appended with a wry attempt at humor. "You from around 'ere, are you, sir?"

"My parents were," Godwin said, not looking at him. "I'm on convalescent leave, you see. Came to visit them today. But when I got there . . . Ruins. Rubble." He gave a shrug.

"Bastards, aren't they?" the warden said with enormous feeling. "Ruddy bastards! Well, I think we can go down now and join the others."

But his last word was cut short even as he and Godwin made to do so.

A salvo of bombs was being shed by an aircraft driven off the course of the main raid, perhaps evading a searchlight—now a dozen were weaving back and forth overhead—or chased by one of the pitifully few night fighters the RAF could muster to zero in on the attackers as darkness thickened. Jettisoned or aimed, those bombs were doing damage. The noise was like the crushing sound of a giant's boots as he marched over the fragile, contemptible creations of humanity.

"Down!" Godwin yelled, and hurled himself flat on the pavement, bringing the warden with him.

A vast detonation rent the air, and even before their tortured eardrums recovered from the blast, their exposed skins were peppered with tiny fragments of masonry. That one had struck within fifty yards or so, probably in the street the fleeing crowd had left mere minutes before.

And the rumble of collapsing walls was followed by a scream.

"Greer! Greer! *Where's my Greer?*"

Here, fighting her way back up the staircase without her baby, was the mother of the family Godwin had singled out. She clutched at his arm, whimpering.

"Greer, my oldest!" she babbled. "Myrna's there and Bette's there and Merle's there—but where's my Greer? Where's my oldest? I did wake her up, I swear I did, but she was in the other room and—*ohhh!*"

Her coherent words dissolved into sobbing.

Simultaneously, a sound of crunching mixed with the hiss of a gas main taking fire indicated that a block of flats just out of sight was being destroyed: maybe hers.

"I'll find her for you," Godwin promised. He spun on his heel, the ache from his leg wound instantly forgettable.

"Stop! Stop!" shouted the warden, who was portly and middle-aged and exempted from military service. After a pause to decide whether he might safely so address an officer, he added, "You bloody fool!"

But Godwin was already rounding the corner. There was nothing for it but to set out after him, at a waddling run.

The sky glowed redder and the air grew dirtier and the stench blew fouler and there were more and more horrible, hideous, gut-wrenching *crump-crump-crump* sounds as the metal birds overhead shat their loads of ruin on what had once been the richest city of the planet.

Godwin's thin leather shoe-soles reported every lump and bump of the rubble-strewn road. Also his trousers were of a coarse emergency material and rubbed his calves and he had dropped his gloves somewhere on the way and his underpants chafed his crotch and his silly stiff-peaked cap kept trying to fall off, although he managed to keep it in position with reflex tosses of his head until he was back in the street where the temporary bus stop stood. There he lost it as he stumbled over an unseen block of débris that did his injured leg no good at all.

Still, he was able to pull himself upright and survey the scene.

The bomb had fallen, not on the tenement from which the family with film stars' names had come pouring out (what would the baby be called, who wearing only a vest was obviously a boy? Cary? Gary? Van?), but straight through the roof of the next building but one, and had exploded at basement level. Walls which had been upright canted insanely around him, uttering creaks and showers of dust. Taking a single step seemed like a terrifying commitment, not solely because glass and brickwork crunched at every move, reminding him of the image of the trampling giant (but the aircraft were swerving away, lightened and quickened by the disposal of their bomb loads), but because those tall façades of masonry had been rendered precarious, the element of choice removed from them in favor of something random, something hazardous, something impervious to reason and to prayer . . .

Godwin had never been so exhilarated in his life.

One wall in particular was clearly about to collapse: the frontage of the building where (if she still lived) little Greer must be hiding. Apart from having shed all its glazing, it was rayed by huge irregularly slanting cracks, springing from door- and window-corners. It was dark; the darkness stank; the air was dry and dried out the mouth, the gullet, the guts of Godwin Harpinshield so that like a desiccated sketch for a reed pipe he sang unbearable chants of delicious agony to the basso continuo of the falling bombs and the rising shells and the tormented city.

Transfixed by the experience, he was a collected butterfly on the stark, bare mounting board of time.

A flare, or a flash from reflected searchlights, lent a gleam of whiteness to the world. Abruptly he saw a child clearly in the maw of the sandbagged entry: skeletally thin limbs poking out from a cotton nightdress

much too small for her, peaked on her rib-ridged chest
by fistlike breasts achieving the status of a nipple/knuck-
le, an O-wide mouth and O-wide eyes, obviously
screaming . . . but the sound was drowned out by
other and more awful noise. Now the building adjacent
was alight from basement to attic and the flames created a blowtorch roar, the hiss of a dragon closing on
his virgin prey. So much oxygen was being sucked from
the air, it was growing hard to breathe.

Calm, Godwin assessed his chances, surveying the
piles of rubble. The odds were bad but not prohibitive.
Decision reached, he darted forward with the erratic,
jinking run of a rugby three-quarter, treating the obstacles as though they were only opposing players. And
the wall to the left, and then the wall to the right, began
to buckle, dislodging bricks *clunk, clunk.*

"Stop!" howled the warden following Godwin. And,
invoking the most powerful charm he knew: "Stop,
sir!"

Godwin paid no heed. His leg was hurting worse at
every step, but it would last long enough. Greer rushed
toward him. He seized her in both arms, spun around
and fled back the way he had come, carrying her as
lightly as a mere football. Only twenty yards to the corner . . . ten . . .

The shock of yet another bomb, falling a street or so
away, was too much for the wall of the burning tenement. It opened brick-dribbling jaws at first-floor level,
sliding, grinding, settling in a torrent of sparks, a wave
of flames.

"Hurry!" the warden screamed, and Godwin lunged
forward as though hurling his body across a goal line,
the child thrust out before him at full stretch. He was
not quite fast enough to save himself. A chunk of masonry hit him on the right arm, and he heard as much
as felt the bones snap. But before pain wiped away consciousness he was able to register that he had saved the
little girl, who could, he now realized, be no older than
ten. She was staring at him by the flamelight with huge,

dark, somehow hungry eyes, as though to eat the very image of her rescuer.

She was there also, with her mother and sisters and baby brother, in the crowd that lined the pavement to watch heroes arriving for the following week's royal investiture. The high iron railings before the palace yard had been taken away to build fighters, but loyal citizens would not have dreamed of venturing uninvited into the grounds.

It was curious, Godwin thought as he marched smartly forward at the calling of his name and gave an awkward salute with his left arm because the right was in a sling—it was curious and also somehow a little disappointing that this king was not majestically tall as children would have wished, but only of average height, and that his queen should be of such a comfortable housewifely plumpness . . . But it was a moment to be treasured forever when those thin, uncertain fingers lifted the George Medal—named after a saint, and himself—from the red velvet cushion on which it was proffered by an equerry and pinned it below the wings which he himself did not display, even though he wore the uniform of a Marshal of the Royal Air Force.

"Congratulations, Squadron Leader," he said. The promotion had been gazetted while Godwin lay in the hospital. "By the way, yours is an unusual name. Irish, one presumes?"

"Yes, Your Majesty." A little dryly, a little deprecatingly. "I've always been told—excuse me—we were descended from the High Kings of Erin."

That provoked a wan smile. "An older house than mine! Whose members had the good sense to go out of business before they invented modern warfare."

It was known that there was a miniature factory in the palace, where bombs and shells were made by royal hands.

"I understand you lost your parents in a recent raid," the king continued after a brief hesitation.

"Yes, sir."

"I'm very sorry."

Pause. There were others waiting. Time to take a pace backward and again give the wrong-handed salute. It was returned, but distractedly. Another medal was on the red velvet pad; another name was being announced. It was over.

But of course he had to make it seem much more dramatic for Mrs. Gallon and her children and all the strangers who came swarming around him as he regained the street. The little girls were dressed in their best, and it was pitiful, but they had at least been thoroughly scrubbed and their well-washed hair shone in the sunlight and they shared a waiflike prettiness which, if one looked hard, might be discerned also behind the tired mask of their mother's features. He told them all about the ceremony, with a garnish of invented detail because truly he had not paid much attention to the furnishings or decorations of the room he had been in; he had looked only at the king and queen.

Finally he said he had to go, and saluted Mrs. Gallon, who giggled and blushed, and rumpled the hair of each of the girls, leaving Greer to last. But she was not content to be patted on the head. She seized his hand as it approached and pulled him down and put her other arm behind his neck and astonished him with her precocity by kissing him open-mouthed, thrusting her tiny tongue between his teeth.

"Greer!" her mother said in horror. "You mustn't do that to the gentleman! I'm sorry, sir—she's a real terror, that one, a proper caution! I'm sure *I* don't know where she gets it from!"

But the last thing Godwin wanted was for her to stop. The contact was incredibly erotic; sensation lanced down his spine like electric current, triggering every reflex on its way.

Must, though. Must! He visualized headlines about indecent assault in broad daylight. Never mind that she committed it.

Contenting himself with one answering passage of his tongue against hers, which conveniently trapped a trace of saliva that might otherwise have glistened on his chin—and irrelevantly remembering that he had expected to have a mustache—he hoisted Greer off her feet for a one-armed hug and grinned as he lowered her again.

Thinking of infection, and countless thousands of girls of this generation who would be given complete sets of false teeth for a twenty-first-birthday present.

"Not to worry, Mrs. Gallon!" he said in the heartiest tone he could conjure up. "I'm sure it's kindly meant. You take care of yourself, young Greer, and one day you'll make some man extremely happy, I'm convinced of it. And now"—he glanced around—"I really must go. There's my bus!"

Everybody knew buses were too precious to miss, these days. It was the right excuse. He went away.

RETURNING home, he landed his Fouga Magistère—his current favorite of the available two-seater jet aircraft—at Stag Lane aerodrome and drove into central London in his Lamborghini Urraco. There was a reggae program playing on Capital Radio which served to distract him during the occasional traffic snarl-ups, but as ever he made excellent time; even the cowboys seemed reluctant to dice with a machine wearing that much horsepower. He dropped it off for a tune-up, wash, and polish at the usual garage and completed his journey on foot, raising the collar of his coat against a gray drizzle, carefully shielding his medal and the newspaper cutting which authenticated it.

So far nobody, he noted as he turned the corner of his home street, had turned up to collect the Jaguar Mark X which had been pushed into the curb when it ran out of petrol . . . how long ago? Long enough for piles of rubbish—ice-lolly wrappers, fish-and-chip paper, empty soft-drink cans—to have accumulated against its wheels. Its windscreen wipers and wing mirrors had been pilfered and kids had tried to start a spectacular fire by setting a match to cardboard piled under its tank, but by then it had been too dry to yield the hoped-for pyrotechnics; they had only managed to blister some of the paint.

Shame about that.

The rain was penetrating and the wind was chilly. As soon as he reached the upper floor of the house where he rented a room, he realized that what he needed was some bright warm sunshine. Carefully closing the door behind him—not that, in fact, even the old woman who owned the house and was overfond of gin and could be heard, until he shut the door, laughing her silly head off at some nondescript television comedy show, could have interrupted him without invitation . . . because that was one of the conditions—he peeled off his Dunn's tweed hat and his Gannex raincoat (as patronized by a recent prime minister), and then his sweater and jeans and boots and socks and helped himself to a generous measure of José Cuervo tequila, complete with salt and lemon, en route to a refreshing shower. When he came out, sweating just enough not to want to don clothing again for the moment, he felt hungry. He lay down in sunshine, but with his head in shade, and ate a slice or two of smoked salmon with crisp fresh salad, washed down with a foaming mug of pilsner. Satisfied, he lit an El Rey del Mundo petit corona and debated where in his souvenir cabinet to put the George Medal and the accompanying scrap of newspaper dated 20th September 1940, two columns under a common headline saying LOCAL HEROES HONOURED AT PALACE; the left column gave a description of the award ceremony and a list of names, while the right one contained four passport-style photographs, the second of which was captioned *Sqn. Ldr. G. Harpinshield, G.M.* It was an excellent likeness. The photographer had gone to much trouble to capture the contrast between his pale, chiseled features and his dark eyes and hair.

Eventually he concluded the medal would look best next to the Schneider Cup and hung it there, intending to pin the cutting alongside.

Curiously enough, however, he found himself unable to rid his mind, every time he looked at it, of the memory of that scrawny little blond girl who had kissed him with a skill beyond her years. Indeed, the erotic associations were so fierce, he found his hand straying toward his crotch.

Before he reached a decision, however, concerning either where to put the press cutting or whether to masturbate, he was startled by a yawn. And also a little dismayed. It was not ordinary to be overcome in this fashion quite so soon after one of his rewards.

Still, there was no point in trying to resist—or he assumed there wasn't; he had never made the attempt, and most likely never would. A little leeway was always permitted, and this time he used it to fold the press cutting carefully, slip it into an envelope, and pocket it. But that was all the margin he was given. Resigned, he switched off the room.

Surrounded now by stained and faded wallpaper, with cobwebs in the corners and a layer of grease coating the sink which doubled as a washbasin, he lay down on the unmade, creaky, narrow single bed and closed his eyes.

Time to pay.

BOTH of that was mostly Thursdays, but it was obviously a Saturday when he came to himself again, his right calf aching in a manner that made him think of falling bombs and a child with fluffy fair hair, and his mouth and belly sour with a sensation forty-eight foul hours of self-indulgence deep, compound of overeating and overdrinking and far too many cigars. Without even bothering to activate the room again, he made for the sink and emptied his bladder and scrubbed his teeth so hard he made his gums sore, then gulped down a cup of powdered coffee and began to feel halfway normal, apart from the usual strains and bruises.

Catching sight of himself in the room's one fly-specked mirror, he grimaced. He looked more like fifty than his chosen thirty-two. A visit to Irma, therefore. No appointment necessary. His arrival would be taken for granted, as he took for granted the need for it. It was never pleasant, having her work him over, but awareness was burgeoning in his mind that tonight he had a task to perform: one of the tasks he was so superbly good at. He would far rather have taken time out—gone to Bermuda or the Caribbean for a while, to recover from what had been done to his body—but he did, after all, have his George Medal.

Fair do's.

Turning the room back on, he went to the wardrobe and found appropriate clothes: a white bomber jacket with gold stripes, new black trousers, black boots with thick elastic soles. Also on the table beside the enormous circular waterbed were dark glasses and the key to a room at the Global Hotel in Park Lane. Although he had never to his recollection been there, he knew he would be recognized when he arrived; it was part of the pattern.

The room automatically shut itself down as he left. Outside, he found the early-evening weather overcast and damp. A bunch of kids, two black and four white, had taken over the Mark X Jaguar as a playhouse, someone having forced its doors. Oh, well . . .

Only at the end of the street did he realize he had omitted to shave. But there must be a reason for that: style, trendiness . . .

There was always a reason for everything he did, whether or not he understood it.

At one of Bond Street's most fashionable addresses there was *not*—naturally!—a sign to tell the world that here was where the Beautiful People spent most money on being made so. Word of mouth served infinitely better to support Irma's cherished, and fulfilled, ambition.

It being the day it was, nobody but one of her oldest acquaintances (friends? Somehow the concept rang false, but there it was, to be put up with) could have walked in and stated his, or her, requirements. She was, though, awaiting Godwin; they had known each other for quite a while.

It was preferable not to put a number to the years.

She looked him over in the high-ceilinged room, lit with pitiless fluorescents, where she plied her trade. She was a handsome, square-faced, ash-blond woman who had decided to appear forty and lay claim to fifty because of Signe Hasso in *L'Éternel Retour* . . . which, in fact, was the name of her shop. Her hobby, which dated back to the time when she was reading biology at university, was the raising of exotic plants. Currently she had a species which glowed with a rich deep sheen whenever it decided to cross the floor in search of a new location. She had half a dozen trays of earth set out, and electronic gear which provoked the response, and when Godwin came in, three of the things—plump, luscious, like cacti but luminous and far more graceful—were under way from one to another rooting site. The first was ruby-red, the next yellow, and the third shone with a vibrant blue.

"Perfect timing!" Irma crowed as Godwin entered.

"Aren't they darling? Are they not perfectly and entirely darling?"

She spoke with especial fervor. Almost all her clients—for obvious reasons—were forbidden to see and admire her treasures, and a visit from someone who was allowed to witness her achievement was to be exploited to the full.

Godwin, though, was aching from head to toe. Whatever his body had had to put up with recently, it had taken a gigantic toll of his resources. As he stripped off his clothes and prepared to lie down under the apparatus which Irma was marshaling, he could only say curtly, "Yes—very pretty! But what happened to the Regulan plants you had before?"

"Rigelian!" she corrected sharply, pushing him with a firm hand into the right position on the table, which was broad and white and cold, and very hard. "Yes, they were all very well in their way, but they couldn't stand the nitrogen . . . or was it the carbon monoxide? No, that was the ones I had before . . . Oh, never mind!"—with a sketch for a laugh. "They are lovely, these, aren't they?"

"Gorgeous!" he said with feigned enthusiasm, shutting his eyes. "Where are they from?"

"Oh, I don't know! Somewhere interesting, I think . . . What *have* you been doing to yourself?"—as she probed and tested his body tissue. "I hope you've allowed plenty of time, because you don't look in the least like you ought to at your age."

That was a gibe, and he resigned himself to it; it was deserved. It was Irma's talent to correct him so that every time he came back he would always leave here looking precisely as someone of thirty-two ought currently to look.

And not, of course, him alone.

Her mood improved as soon as she set about her work, as always. While she was removing his surplus fat she began to hum, and by the time she got around to erasing his wrinkles—not just from his face, but from every inch of his skin—she was cheerful enough to start boasting.

"Say, know who I had in here yesterday? Bruce Bastard-Bitch of the Claimjumpers! *You* know! This Aussie sick-rock group they're all talking about now! Was he a *mess*! I swear, I don't know what they get up to down under to ruin their bodies in such short order. Of course if they had"—archly—*"guidance . . . !"*

Meantime she was readjusting his hairline to correspond with the present fashion and dehydrating him of a kilo of superfluous fluid. He could feel the tingling sensation as it flowed out through his pores, taking with it the fatigue products accumulated around his strains and bruises. He relaxed, and despite the discomfort began to feel quite sympathetic toward her. Almost, indeed, affectionate.

"I suppose you *do* have to keep up that level of 17-ketosteroids, but it sure plays hell with your follicles," she sighed as she checked his hormone count. It was one of her minor abilities, to be able to sigh at such length. But he tolerated it, just as he did her belief in being guided. It was, after all, one way of putting it . . .

"Now let's do something about the accommodation of that right eye of yours," she continued, shuffling her machines around and bringing to bear one which focused a dim green light on his retina. *"Oh*, yes. Still a bit lazy, just as I thought. Won't take a moment, though . . . What's new with you, by the way?"

"Oh, nothing much . . ." But it was scarcely worth the doing unless there were people he could tell, and there were so few of them. He came out with it directly.

"I won the George Medal for rescuing a kid during the Blitz. I saved her life."

"You never!" But it wasn't a contradiction, only an exclamation. "I always knew you had it in you! Well, well, you actually won a medal! Did you get it from the king in person?"

"Yes. Want me to prove it with a press cutting?"

Already on first recounting it seemed far away and

irrelevant. His eye had been attended to and everything in the room, including the faint reflections on the bright white tiles as the plants wandered from soil tray to soil tray, gleaming amber now and russet and orange, was far too sharply in focus for his comfort. Next, he knew, needles would probe his neck and shoulder muscles, eliminating rheumatoid plaques, and after that she would set about the business of updating him. She was invariably meticulous; every time he left here, he looked exactly as a contemporary thirty-two-year-old should.

But it was not always a pleasant experience.

"A George Medal!" she was repeating, as though to savor the very shape of the words. "Well, well! God, I bet you wish you could go around telling everybody!"

That idea was so patently absurd it was uncomfortable. Rolling over at her insistence so she could insert her needles, he caught sight of the plants again and said with an effort, "They certainly are very pretty, these new things of yours. Where did you say they came from?"

"Oh—one of the planets of Sirius, I think," she answered absently. "Just a second. Don't move, don't even breathe . . . Got it. Ah—yes, Sirius or somewhere. But you should see the big ones I have at home! Taller than me, and *so* graceful! You really ought to drop around some time. What about tonight?"

He knew and she knew what the response was sure to be, but he was glad to be able to say honestly, "I'm afraid not. I'm being called."

"I see. That's why you're here, hm?" she said with affected nonchalance. "Okay, there goes your rheumatism. Now we'll service your face and hands and that'll do."

Her voice betrayed her, though. It must have been a long while since she was called. Clearly she wasn't relishing retirement. Moreover, since she and he dated back to about the same time . . .

But she put a brave face on it, and a moment later as she reorganized his eyebrows she was saying, "I'm going to win a trophy at the Chelsea Flower Show, you know. For gladioli, I think. And tomorrow—I mean on Monday—you'll never guess who's coming for the first time! Candida Bright! You know, the actress who just won the best-of-year award on ITV?"

Not, of course, to enjoy this kind of treatment. Godwin said absently, "When?"

"Oh, last month some time, I think. It was in the papers."

"No, I meant the trophy."

Even before the words were out, he realized how tactless they were. "Soon, let's hope!" he added heartily as she stood back and indicated that he could get up and dress. The addition provoked a wan smile.

She ushered him personally to the door and kissed him on both cheeks before letting him out into the street. As he strode away, she called, "Do remember what I said about dropping by some time, won't you?"

That obliged him to turn around and wave back and thus look at her again. He would much have preferred not to see her as she was with her defenses down: as other people were not privileged to see her, as she should never have been seen at all.

For that insight, too, there was of course a reason.

A proper caution.

THE evening was cool but at least it was dry. God-win drove to the underground car-park in Park Lane and left the Urraco there, jingling the hotel key he had found. Crossing the road, he noticed that the whores and beggars were out in force tonight, though traffic was naturally as light as it always was nowadays. Half a dozen couples of police—one man, one woman—were trying to prevent people being accosted, but it was a job like painting the Forth Bridge. Driven from one spot, the nuisance rematerialized elsewhere a moment later.

Seeing him approach, one of the commissionaires on duty before the Global Hotel reacted alertly. "Good evening, sir!" he exclaimed as he trod on the pad before the automatic sliding doors to save Godwin the fractional delay involved in doing so himself.

"Good evening—ah . . . ?" Godwin said as he slid a pound into the man's white-gloved hand.

"Jackson, sir!"

"Thank you, Jackson."

He walked into the foyer, which at this time of evening was full of customers smartly dressed for an evening on the town. He recognized several people who were household names—actors, politicians, business-men—and was himself recognized, even though he did not recall ever being here before. But that was the way of things in his life.

"No messages, sir!" the girl on the reception desk twinkled at him. "But I reserved your table in our disco, which opens at ten o'clock."

"Thank you, Molly," he said, reading her name off

the badge she wore pinned to her crisp white shirt, and left another pound lying discreetly on the counter.

Glancing around as he turned away, he saw a head of fair hair above a lean, muscular back, and for a second could have imagined . . . but no. It belonged to a young man; when he turned, he revealed a beard. And why should he be paying attention to that kind of thing, anyhow?

All the staff he encountered as he went up to his room—correction: "his" room—beamed at him. Entering it, he discovered awaiting him a bottle of champagne and a basket of fruit, the card accompanying which said they came with the compliments of the management.

He nodded thoughtful approval of all that that implied. In the early days there had sometimes been disasters to sort out. As time passed, this kind of thing had become more and more typical. One might put it down to increasing skill, born of frequent practice.

Or perhaps it was due to something else entirely. There was no means of finding out, so there was no point in worrying about it.

He called room service for caviar, an underdone steak and a tossed salad, and ate quietly on his own, not touching the champagne. He could only drink in the safety of his own home. But he sampled the fruit and found it delicious.

Lighting another of his favorite petit coronas, he went down to the hotel discothèque a few minutes after ten.

This early, it was almost empty apart from staff. Its roof was mirrored at crazy angles. Chairs and tables were grouped to form a horseshoe. In the center was a dais of thick glass, over water kept constantly in motion, on which were reflected lights that constantly changed color. A bar ran down one wall, and at it sat some bored-looking prostitutes tolerated by the management—conceivably because they kicked back a portion of their takings. It was a very stock scene indeed.

The DJ looked bored as he sorted through his supply of tapes and records; the barmen were yawning as though they had only just got up; the women were much too heavily painted, as though expecting to be viewed on stage by people the far side of footlights, not at close quarters. One girl, tawny-skinned and slender, was on the dance floor writhing and gyrating, but she was like the token coin in the collection tray.

"Ah, good evening, sir!" a waitress said, purring up to him. "We have the same table for you as last night and the night before. I'm afraid we weren't expecting you quite so early, so I haven't set out your champagne yet—"

"Coke," he said.

She blinked at him. She was pretty, brown-haired, youthful.

"Coke," he repeated. Her face fell, but she only shrugged and said nothing as she turned away, expecting him—of course—to know which table he had reserved.

Instead, he remained where he was, glancing about him and wondering what he was here for. He knew, of course, in the broadest sense, but the details so far were elusive. There was nothing for it but to wait.

The girl returned, bringing his Coke and also carrying an enormous menu which, as she indicated his table and he sat down at it, she thrust into his hands. He did no more than glance at it, registering that it offered extremely basic food—hamburgers, cheeseburgers, pizza, kebabs—at stratospheric prices . . . not, of course, that that could worry him. But he gave it back to her almost at once with a shake of his head.

"I ate already," he muttered, and leaned back to savor the last of his cigar.

She gave him an extremely puzzled look, but departed with another shrug, and in a little while was seen to be talking with the headwaiter. Both of them kept casting glances in his direction. Godwin ignored them, and very shortly they were distracted as new customers arrived. Within half an hour or so there were twenty people present and four young couples were dancing under the randomly changing lights—and above them. The effect of the reflection from the ripples was colorful and imaginative; he watched it most of the time he was sitting alone.

Now and then he was interrupted by the passage of one or other waiter or waitress, each of whom greeted him cordially and hovered for a while, clearly expecting him to place an order. As each in turn moved away disappointed, they wore identical looks of perplexity.

It grew very warm in the room. One of the girls, who had come in with a fat, father-old escort, took off her blouse and started dancing topless; another, not to be outdone, peeled off her dress and danced in bikini panties, barefooted. Both were young and quite attractive, and for a while Godwin wondered whether he should be interested in them. But neither seemed to show any sign of recognition.

It was not until nearly midnight—by which time the place was crowded and his table, in single occupation and with nothing on it but a half-empty glass of Coke and a clean ashtray, formed the eye of a storm of noise and shouting and feverish activity—that the girl he was expecting turned up.

Two young men, both apparently Arabs, both in impeccable dinner suits incongruously combined with pale fawn headdresses bound with green silk cords, entered ahead of two women: one plump and blond, about thirty, and the other slim and brown-haired but with a streak of silver, very much younger—at most, eighteen. It was she who, glancing around, spotted him and gave a nervous wave and smile behind her companions' backs. She wore yellow satin pants, very tight, and a blue strapless top held up by a ruched elastic insert. On the left of her neck, inexpertly powdered over, there was a strawberry-colored bite mark. She looked tired and ill at ease. But she smiled the instant she caught sight of Godwin, and everything—or almost everything—became clear to him.

One table remained vacant, in a bad position well

away from the dance-floor, and the party was shown to it and at once supplied with a bottle of whisky and a bowl of ice and a syphon of soda, along with dishes of junk food of the kind Godwin had been resolutely refusing since his arrival. Like alcohol, that was something he would only risk in the security of home. He waited another couple of minutes until the group settled down, then rose and approached them with his most leonine strides. Thanks to Irma, his body tingled with vitality, and virtually everyone in the place stared at him as he moved.

The girl started up from her chair in excitement, holding out her hand to seize his as soon as he came in range.

"I'm so glad you're here!" she exclaimed. "Let me introduce my friends! This is Rashad. This is Afif. This is Peggy. This is Godwin!"

He acknowledged them with a succession of cool nods, not letting go of her hand. It was very clear from their expressions that neither Afif—the older—nor Rashad welcomed his intrusion. In fact both looked in a thoroughly bad temper. He sensed storm warnings, but continued anyhow.

"Hello . . . I came over to ask if you'd like to dance with me." Beautifully controlled, his voice lanced through the din.

"Yes, I'd love to! You will excuse me, won't you?"—to Rashad, who was clearly her partner for the evening, wherever it had begun.

"No," he said.

Startled, she stared at him, poised half out of her chair.

He pointed at the dance floor. Some quiet persuasion from the management had removed from it the girls who were going topless and obliged them to dress again, but two or three who were up there now were in shorts and halters or strapless dresses slit to the thigh.

"No," he said again. "I have bought you for tonight. You have been paid for. If you dance, you will dance with me or with my brother."

The brother nodded firm agreement. Blond Peggy looked a trifle alarmed, but did her best to conceal her reaction.

Godwin planted the knuckles of both fists on the table and leaned toward Rashad.

"I asked the lady if she'd like to dance with me and she said yes," he stated in level tones. "She said yes. I don't care how you treat women in the slave markets of wog-land, but in this country they are not for buying and selling. They are people. Got that? Now let's go and dance," he concluded, turning to the girl again.

Rashad's hand flashed across the table and seized her by the wrist.

"You will do as you are told!" he hissed.

"Let go—you're hurting!" she cried.

By now the attention of half the room was on them. Most of the dancers had checked in mid-movement and were staring this way; eyes wide, lips apart, they were visibly hungry for something out of the ordinary run of events, and if it was violent they would be most pleased.

It was not going to turn out that way.

Three tall male members of the staff converged, two to take station either side of Godwin, one to bend deferentially over the Arabs' table and say, "Is this gentleman disturbing you?"

Rashad uttered an Arabic curse and made as though to spit. The deferential one turned to Godwin.

"I believe the manager would like a word with you, sir. This way, if you please."

After what Irma had done to him, Godwin was well aware he could have broken all three of them into small pieces and scarcely been out of breath at the end of it, but somehow this did not feel like the right response. Shrugging, he let himself be led through a door set inconspicuously at the end of the bar, and instantly he was in another world: one of hustle and bustle, of deliveries and shouted orders, of dust and litter and junk to be concealed from the gaze of the clientèle. A few yards along a dim-lit corridor, and they entered the manager's office: a shabby room with functional furniture, an old-fashioned desk, telephones, filing cabinets, a worn rug on a concrete floor.

The manager, a balding man of fifty-odd, didn't even glance up as he spoke on Godwin's entrance.

"I don't know what your game is, chum, but I don't like it. I'm not even sure you're you, and not your twin brother. Last night and the night before, you come in here like the original big spender, you make with the tips and the champagne, you generally make yourself welcome. Tonight you don't eat, you don't drink, you don't dance, you sit there like a bloody statue *and*, to crown it all, you make waves with Prince Afif and Prince Rashad—"

One of the phones on his desk buzzed; it was an internal one. He barked at it, "Yes?" And listened.

"The hell you say," he said after a while. "That's exactly what we don't need!"

Cradling the receiver, he stared directly at Godwin for the first time.

"They marched out!" he snapped. "Said this wasn't the way they expected to be treated! I hope you're bloody satisfied!"

"What do you expect me to do if your rich chums behave like slave dealers?" Godwin countered.

"I don't give a damn what you do so long as it doesn't fuck up my operation!" He pulled himself to his feet; he overtopped Godwin by a good three inches.

"I gather you have a room in the hotel. Go to it! Get some beddy-byes! And don't come back in my disco, hear? Not until you're prepared to act like a customer again instead of a specter at the bloody feast! Christ, what do you expect me to do—carry you because you spent so much here already you ran out of money? It won't work on me, chummy, if that is your game! I've had 'em all in here, and I keep the ones who can afford it. And only those! Now you get lost, okay?" To one of the heavies he added, "Show him back to the foyer. And I mean show him! Don't turn him loose to 'lose his way' and sneak back into the disco!"

Meekly Godwin let himself be shown, knowing what was in store.

He just had time, eluding his escort, to vanish through the door marked *Gentlemen* before the pangs of punishment descended. There was one astonished young man in the toilet—barely more than a boy—who summed up his condition in a single glance and hurried away . . . and was wrong. Contrary to appearances, Godwin was not drunk enough to vomit, though his paleness and unsteady gait combined to give that impression.

He was simply suffering, and resigned to the fact. He had, after all, messed up his assignment . . . one of the sort he was good at.

In a bolted cubicle he struggled not to resist the pangs, recognizing them as just. But repressing the moans called forth from him cost all his energy, and when it was over he had to sit with head in hands for a long while before he dared venture forth again.

He used the time well, though, and made plans.

Miraculously, it appeared that no one had remembered to get at Jackson. Emerging cautiously into the hotel lobby, Godwin put on the boldest face he could contrive, and strolled toward the entrance as though to glance at the weather. The commissionaire leaped to attention.

"Going out, sir?"

"Not right away," Godwin said musingly, and contrived to slide a fiver into the man's hand. "But . . . Well, you saw Prince Rashad and Prince Afif leave some time ago with a couple of girls?"

"Oh, yes! With Peggy and Gorse. I called them a cab."

"Well, I'm going to be in the lounge bar for a while"—with a jerk of his head. "I'd like to know when they come back. I take it they will come back? They have rooms here?"

"The Imperial Suite on the second floor," Jackson confided. He had made the money vanish without so much as a rustle.

"Fine. I'll sit where I can see you reflected in that glass door," Godwin said, having rapidly checked several possibilities in his mind's eye. "Give me a signal—wave your arm up and down, or something—as soon as you recognize them. Okay?"

"Will do," Jackson said, and Godwin headed for the lounge.

It was almost two hours before the signal came. Thirty cabs had drawn up—for want of any better way to pass the time, Godwin had kept score—and this was the thirty-first. The lounge barman was reading a newspaper and trying not to yawn; the lights were lowered in the foyer; outside, the last of the beggars had quit for the night.

Godwin rose to his feet with electric rapidity and strode out through the automatic doors so fast they would not have had time to open for him. Jackson, though, was already treading on the sensor pad against the arrival of the princes and their women. The taxi was drawing away. Godwin shouted commandingly, "Hang on, driver! I want you!"

Obediently the woman—for it was a woman at the wheel—braked and reversed.

The girl who had been identified by the peculiar name of Gorse was red-eyed and looked as though she had been crying. Peggy was attempting to comfort her. Both the brothers wore expressions of thundercloud rage and were talking to one another in rapid Arabic, paying no more attention to the girls than to make sure they were not trying to cut and run.

The moment they recognized Godwin, they halted in their tracks and flinched away from him. He closed on them with his fists raised to elbow height, wider apart than the width of his body, and the eyes of each fixed, fascinated, on one fist.

"I told you," he said mildly. "I don't care what you get up to in wog-land, but here we don't buy and sell women!"

And instead of punching, he kicked, leaping into the air like a ballet dancer. He caught Rashad first just below the left kneecap and the man crumpled with a yell; then he took Afif in the crotch and strode between the pair of them with one hand poised to catch Gorse by the elbow. With his other hand he hauled open the taxi's door, and seconds later they were safely inside. Reflex made the driver start up the instant the door shut.

"Hey, I say!" she shouted over her shoulder. "I don't like what you just done! You get right out of this cab again, now! Or else I'll call a copper, understand?"

But before she could brake to a halt, Godwin said, "They were going to sell her as a white slave!"

Prompt on cue, the girl crumpled against his shoulder and began to utter huge gut-wrenching sobs.

Before the driver could say anything else Godwin gave her his address and leaned back, stroking Gorse's soft dark hair with its incongruous silver streak as though he were comforting a little child.

So far the whole episode had gone so smoothly he was already on the verge of being bored.

WHEN they were nearly at their destination Gorse sat up without warning and said slowly and clearly, "Please stop. I think I'm going to be sick."

Godwin tapped on the glass partition behind the driver, who understood instantly and pulled in at the curb. Deftly he opened the door and thrust her head out just far enough, keeping his other arm around her to steady her. She uttered a gush of liquid that made the air stink of gin.

Wiping her chin with a handkerchief, he sat her back and closed the door again, and they completed their journey without further incident.

In his home street all but two of the lamps were out. She shivered noticeably as he helped her to the ground, having already passed the cab fare plus a generous tip to the driver. Slowly, through her alcoholic fog, she registered the high-piled rubbish in the gutters, the derelict cars, the dark faces of the houses where many windows had been broken and mended, after a fashion, with cardboard or sheets of plastic.

"What have you brought me here for?" she demanded between a cry and a sob.

"It's where I live," he answered, taking her arm and guiding her roughly up the steps of his home. She tried to rebel, tried to hang back—but a fresh bout of nausea overcame her, and this time instead of spurting out, her vomit dribbled, staining the front of her clothes.

Godwin waited with forced patience until the spasm passed, then urged her indoors. "You're not going anywhere in that state," he muttered. But she scarcely paid attention. She was gesturing at herself, shuddering.

"I didn't mean to make such a mess of myself!" she wailed. "I'm so sorry, I'm so ashamed, I'm such a fool!"

"Right."

He got her up the stairs and into his room, turning it on as he opened the door. She was too befuddled with drink to notice its details, though he himself was rather pleased with them: his usual waterbed, some wall-sized enlargements of erotic pen-and-wash drawings by the French artist Bertrand, several more wardrobes than usual, and a cabinet of perfectly clear glass around the shower, bidet, and toilet bowl. Also the towels were black, a highly suitable color.

Quiet music began, intermingled with the wash of waves on a beach, and the air was warm and fresh and the lamps, when they came on, shed the color of moonlight in irregular patches.

Not bad.

But he had other preoccupations. He said, "Get out of those filthy clothes."

She had begun to cry again as they came upstairs. The brusqueness of his command snapped her back to awareness. She stared at him with a hurt, little-girl look.

"I said get out of them! They reek of vomit!"

"But—but I only bought them day before yesterday! This is my best gear! I can't just . . ."

The words tailed away as she gazed down at herself and realized just how much of a mess she had created. Before she could recover, he reached out with careful precision and tore the garments away from her: rr-rip, rrr-rr-rip. He balled up the fabric and flung it in the direction of a waste bin.

Her sandals had come off along with her satin trousers, so now all she wore was a pair of white panties, also—as she realized when she noticed his glare of distaste—soiled. She whimpered with self-loathing.

"Get in there and clean yourself," he said, pointing at the glass cabinet.

"But . . . !" She stared for a drink-extended moment at the clear glass walls; the door stood wide. Then she reasoned out that on the one hand there was no alternative, and on the other she could scarcely be more humiliated than she was already. Sullen, tears still trickling down from her red-rimmed eyes, she obeyed: emptied her bowels into the pan, flushed the mess away, squatted on the bidet and scrubbed as though trying to punish herself.

"Here," he said, entering the compartment and handing her a glass half full of cloudy white fluid. "Drink this."

She obeyed as though he **were** a doctor and she a patient totally committed to his care. When the glass was empty, he took it back and threw her a towel.

"Dry yourself."

"Have you—have you something I can put on?" she dared to whisper.

"Where do you think you're going?"

He turned his back with deliberate contempt and, waiting for her to follow him out of the glass cage, sipped at a ballon of 1858 Armagnac, which had lost all its vinosity and tasted—and smelled—solely of the oak casks in which it had been matured prior to bottling. The flavor and the bouquet were unique; there was no other liquor like this in the world.

Behind him he heard her crying cease. When she stepped back into the main room, the towel wrapped around her body and tucked in above her breasts, her eyes were sparkling.

"It's incredible! What was it you gave me? I feel fine again!"

"That's what it's for."

"But it's amazing! I never heard of any medicine that could do that!"

"I'm not surprised," he grunted. And wasn't; it was nowhere on sale. Nowhere on Earth, at any rate.

Better or not, though, next moment her face fell. Her gaze had lit on the bundle of cloth he had torn from her.

"That was all I had to wear," she said timidly. "All

my other clothes are at the—the house where I rent a room. Please lend me something so I can go home!"

"No."

She stared at him like a child astonished by a promised punishment which had suddenly turned out to be real. Her lips trembled on the brink of renewed sobs.

He said harshly, "How much of tonight were you expecting to spend at home, you little tart?"

"But I—but I . . . !"

Her last resistance crumbled. She dropped forward on her knees, her head in her hands, and the storm of sobbing which racked her this time was cathartic. Easing his way to a chair, he cajoled her gently closer so that she could rest her forehead on his lap while he stroked her hair, and piece by piece he assembled her story.

Half of it was, predictably, a tissue of lies.

She was eighteen. Her parents had divorced when she was so small she could scarcely remember her father, and into the bargain she hated the name he had bequeathed her—"Simpkins! I mean honestly, who wants to be called Simpkins?"—along with her given name, which was Dora— "Isn't it the bloody end? Dora Simpkins!"

Gorse was a nickname from school which she felt suited her. Currently she was looking for an adoptive surname to go with it. School was an extremely expensive private boarding school near Kenley, in Surrey, not because her father had been rich—he was supposedly a ne'er-do-well and gambler with more charm than persistence—nor because her mother had inherited money. On the contrary, although she had brought up her daughter single-handed, luckily having no other children to worry about, she came from an out-and-out working-class background and had clawed her way to financial success by any means to hand.

"I'm following in her footsteps," Gorse said viciously. "And Granny's as well, though she's dead now."

"Explain." He had let his hand wander from her hair to her nape; in a little while it would travel to her shoulders. Then he would lift her into his lap like a tired child, and explore the rest of her body. The rhythm he was employing was designedly hypnotic; every now and again he checked it for frequency against her pulse, which he felt on the side of her neck. It was slowing in a reassuring manner. There was going to be no trouble with this one. None at all.

"Mum was a call girl," Gorse said sleepily. "She never said so straight out, but that's the only way she could possibly have met people like the ones she knows: MPs, company directors, television executives, artists, actors, poets . . . And she was only taking after Granny, same as me. I'm not supposed to know about it, but Granny was on the streets. Had to be. Granddad was captured in the war and died in a prison camp, and she had five children to look after. They were taken into care eventually and Mummy doesn't know what became of her brother and sisters. All split up. Scattered. Then Gran died and something happened to the records—I think a bomb or something fell on the place where they were stored and they all got burnt. She advertised a few times but nothing happened . . ."

This was of no particular interest. Godwin steered her back to the main line.

Having led a colorful life, her mother was persuaded by a literary friend to try her hand at writing. Scornful at first, because she was effectively uneducated, she finally yielded, and her stories and her books of memoirs—suitably censored—proved financially successful. More and more she cared about her writing; less and less she had time for her daughter. She sent her to that expensive boarding school for, she claimed, the child's own benefit.

"Hers!" Gorse said contemptuously. "Meant she could go gallivanting off to Hollywood and places and make lots of money and screw lots of handsome young men!"

Hollywood in fact was where she was at present, and

had been for two months on a scriptwriting assignment. She had left at the end of the Easter holidays, even though this summer term her daughter was due to face entrance exams for university.

But there was something Gorse wasn't admitting. Being left wholly on her own to confront the stress of those exams was less than an adequate excuse for doing what she'd done. He coaxed her up on his lap and fondled her breasts, letting her murmur secretly against his ear as the warm breezes wafted off a nonexistent ocean and the music sank to a level as faint as its own echoes.

Oh. Acid. He might have guessed.

When she was fourteen, some spoiled upper-class bitch in the top form, thinking to show off as "clever" and "sophisticated," brought back a few tabs of LSD and gave them to those of the junior girls she had a crush on, or vice versa. Gorse had begged one and been given it.

Which through a long and tortuous chain of associated self-justifications purported to explain why, immediately before her exams, she had run off to London determined to see some "real life" and wound up being given a room in a house chiefly occupied by prostitutes under the direction of a pimp with family connections or at any rate contacts in the Global Hotel. He had advanced her what felt like an awful lot of money—to someone confined for three-quarters of the year in a boarding school, a thousand pounds must still sound like a small fortune—and made it very clear that he expected repayment in full, and shortly. That was not all he had given her, moreover. Modeling herself, consciously or unconsciously, on the girl who had brought acid to school, she had accepted several offers of this and that and the other, not only from him but also from other girls in the house.

All very typical. Godwin repressed the urge to yawn and turned her around on his lap so he could caress her clitoris. He made her come almost at once, and while she was still gazing at him in disbelief as though she had never before met a man prepared to concentrate on pleasuring instead of simply using her, he rose to his feet with both arms around her, as casually as though she weighed nothing, and dumped her into bed. The lights dimmed automatically as he joined her a moment later, having discarded his clothes in a few swift movements, and thereafter for half an hour he concentrated on exploiting her capacity for orgasm. It was extensive. She was purring when she went to sleep.

As soon as she had dropped off he stole out of bed again and sat for a while in the chair he had left, pondering his ideal course of action. It took only a short while to reach his decision. Then he made the requisite arrangements.

After that he should have felt the warm satisfaction of a job well done. To a limited extent he did, but it was all the same a trifle disappointing. He would have preferred a more demanding assignment—perhaps one which would have lasted days, or better yet weeks, rather than one which promised to be complete in at most forty-eight hours. It was frankly boring to have become so good at his work. And what was he to look forward to as a reward? Half a dozen possibilities flickered through his mind, but he dismissed almost all of them at once. One did linger, but because it was over-ambitious and must involve great suffering he hesitated to settle on it: who'd want to win World War III?

Well, maybe he would reach a decision when the time came. Several of his very best memories stemmed from a spur-of-the-moment choice.

Having made sure that the room would be in the correct conformation for the morning, he sat and waited, sleep not being essential for him in this mode.

WHEN he woke her, placing a glass of orange juice beside the bed with a deliberately loud noise, she saw him first as she opened her eyes and stretched, and gave a sleepy smile. Then she registered the rest of what was in view.

Two seconds . . . three . . . her face crumpled and she was weeping and diving for shelter under the coverlet.

"*Now* what the hell's wrong with you?" he barked, pulling it aside. She curled into a fetal ball, striving to shut the world out with her palms. But she had to choose between eyes and ears and preferred eyes, so he was able to reach her without shouting.

Also she was moaning, and the moaning made a confused kind of sense.

"When will they stop? Won't they ever stop? Oh, *God!*"

"What?" And when, having waited long enough, he had had no answer, he forced her to sit up and pulled her hands away from her face.

"Are you feeling hung over or something?" he demanded, not because he didn't know the answer to that one. "Here, drink this! It's fresh!"

The urge to resist departed from her. Dull-faced, slow-moving as a marionette, she accepted the glass and cradled it in both hands, trying not to look anywhere except straight at it. She said after sipping it, "It just goes on and on. I never thought it would last so long. It's driving me insane."

"What?" he said again.

"The flashes!"

"Sounds as though you could do with coffee and a proper breakfast," he said, straightening and turning away. "If you mean an acid flash, you're not having one right now."

She jerked her head full upright and stared to her left, across the field-sized expanse of the waterbed. The sun beamed down on sparkling white coralline sand beyond the window; the air was full of the hushing of gentle waves.

"It can't be real!" she breathed. "It can't be!"

"Have it your way," he sighed. "I'm putting sugar in your coffee whether you take it or not. No milk."

"I don't usually—" She bit the words off. "Thank you," she amended meekly, as though she had been taking stock of herself and realized that some quickly assimilable energy was advisable. But her eyes were fixed, like a hypnotized chicken's, on cloudless blue sky and foaming combers.

The spell did not break until he brought her a mug of coffee and a platter of scrambled eggs dotted with the sharp green of fresh-cut chives. She took the former and looked at the latter with regret.

"I never eat breakfast," she said defiantly.

"Tomorrow you can do what you like. For the rest of your life you can do what you like, same as me. Today you do as you're told. It will be the last time."

Uncertainly she set aside the empty glass and let him put a fork into her hand. But she made no attempt to start eating.

"I don't understand. What do you mean, I can do what I like?"

"What did you think you were going to do when you ran away from school? End up as a drunken floozie sucking off impotent Arabs?"

"You're disgusting!"

"Not half as disgusting as you were when you vomited all over yourself last night."

She said flatly, "Now I know I am still getting flashes. I remember that. But either that isn't true or this isn't. I remember the horrible dark street. I remember the way my feet squelched in muck when I got out of the taxi. I remember the stink. It can't have been when I was coming here. Unless you took me somewhere while I was asleep."

"You're here, where I brought you. Eat those eggs before they get cold."

Mechanically she began to ply her fork. The first mouthful reminded her of the existence of appetite, and she cleared the plate. Her face, though, remained set in an unhappy frown, and between bites she cast cautious glances at the sunny view from the window, as though challenging the scene to go away.

She said finally, "It must cost millions. So why here?"

"Because I want it, and it doesn't." He took away the empty plate. "Get up, go pee and shit and take a shower, and get dressed."

"What do I put on?" she snapped back. "You ruined the only clothes I had with me!"

"Look in that wardrobe," he said, gesturing. "Plenty there to fit you. But hurry up."

Very reluctantly, gathering the bed sheet for covering, she complied. But instead of heading for the toilet, she could not resist the temptation to walk to the window and stare out, raising one hand to shield her eyes against the brilliant sunshine.

"You don't like it?"

"It's beautiful! I just don't understand . . ." Her voice trailed away.

"You wouldn't like to live somewhere like this?"

"What a hope!" She gave a harsh laugh and turned her back to the window.

"Is that what you thought you were heading for when you ran away? I'm still waiting for an answer from the last time I asked."

"Oh, God . . . I didn't know what I wanted. I still don't know what I want. What the hell difference does it make? Nobody ever gets what he wants. She wants. Whatever the hell." Dispirited, she cast the sheet aside and stepped into the glass compartment.

"Stop staring at me, you bloody voyeur," she added as she turned to sit down on the toilet. "Much more of this and I'll be sorry I didn't stick with the Arabs."

"Much more of this and you'll have to. I'm still waiting for my answer!"

She disregarded him. There was a mirror so sited that by twisting around she could catch sight of her reflection. Raising her fingers to run them comb-fashion through her tousled hair, she said more to herself than to him, "Oh, God, I do look a mess. How the hell am I going to explain when I get home?"

"If it's true your mother was a call girl, you won't have any trouble explaining."

She jerked her head around to glare at him, flushing.

"Where she lives isn't my home! I mean the place I'm living now. Where all my things are."

"There are always more things."

"It may be all right for you, but some of us have to bloody earn them!"

"Some of us don't. You could be one of them. No need for you to go crawling back to some foul-mouthed pimp and beg forgiveness for having run out on the rich client he stuck you with last night."

Godwin carefully refrained from hinting or even implying what was fundamentally obvious: that the taint of masochism already infected the core of her being. It was a standard precondition. Instead, he added—before she had the chance for a retort—"That can't have been what you were looking for! There must be something you're good at! Some talent you've always wanted to turn into a career! *Something!*"

With elaborate casualness, making believe she was not in this exposed and vulnerable setting, she tore and slowly folded sheets of paper from the roll and wiped herself. Not looking anywhere near him, she said finally, "I want to be a designer."

"What sort of designer?"

"Textiles. Wallpapers. That sort of thing. I think I've got it in me. And I've always thought how marvelous it would be to walk into somewhere—a four-star restau-

rant, some rich person's home, a set in a film studio—
and see my work all over the walls!"

Her voice was taking on the color of genuine enthusiasm.

"And not just on the walls. On the floor too, perhaps. The carpets or the tiles. The curtains, the furniture, the clothes!"

Godwin gave a thoughtful nod. Yes, this one was
going to take. It was an absolutely flawless combina-
tion. One push in the right direction—the investment,
as he had estimated, of about forty-eight hours' worth
of his time—and the job would be complete. Of course,
there was the usual matter of convincing her about
her new reality, but that was Hermann's problem, not
his, and after that it would be plain sailing.

Once again he found himself hankering after something at least a trifle more demanding. But that was
pointless.

She had flushed the toilet and was stepping into the
shower. Checking, she glanced back.

"You must think I'm an idiot. Don't you?"

"No, if you've got it in you, it can start tomorrow. Or
even today."

She curled her lip at him.

"No, I'm serious."

He was sitting in a chair with splayed metal legs; if
he tilted it far enough back, he could open the nearer of
the wardrobes. At full stretch he slid its door aside.

"When you've finished showering, you can take your
pick of this lot. Do you like the idea?"

She was staring in disbelief. "But—but aren't those
terribly expensive?"

"What makes you think so?"

"Well, they look like . . ." Eyes wide, lips wet because she had unconsciously licked them, she hesitated.
"They look like the latest fashion."

He jerked a brown tweed coat off its hanger and held
it where she could read the label. It said Peasmarsh.
Her eyes rounded.

"I'll take you to see Hugo & Diana later on and get you a complete new outfit."

"You know them?"

"I know a lot of people."

"But I can't possibly afford—!"

"There are always more things." This time he said it with the platitudinous flatness of a self-evident truth.

"I still can't afford—"

"Who's asking you to? Get in that shower and make the most of it."

Still she lingered, her eyes fixed on the ranked clothes. He said after a while, "You have exactly three choices. You put on your rags and tatters, stained with vomit, and return to the whorehouse you came from. Or you do the same and go whining and begging back to your mother, or the school she sent you to, which amounts to the same thing, because you said last night your mother will be in America for at least another week. Or you can do as you like for the rest of your life, which will be long and healthy. It's up to you. But I shall in any case leave here in approximately five minutes, and whether I go where I'm next going on my own is for you to decide. At all events I shall certainly not let you stay here by yourself, even if it means putting you out in the street with nothing on. Is that clear?"

He spoke with deliberate harshness. She drank in every word, and the moment he had finished, walked toward him and laid her right hand on his arm, smiling.

"Do you know something?"

"What the hell is it this time?"

"I've never told anybody this before. Never in my whole life. Not my best friends."

"Then it probably isn't worth saying. Get on and have a shower like I told you!"

She stood her ground, clutching his hand tightly now.

"No, you've got to listen! Sometimes I've dreamed— sometimes I've tried with all my heart and soul to believe—that my father who ran away when I was still a baby *wasn't* my father. That one day it would turn out the real one could never acknowledge me because he was married and a very important figure in politics or something, maybe even someone royal, only now his wife was dead and he could come and tell me the truth and he'd take charge of me and straighten out my life"—the words were coming in a torrent now—"and *be masterful* and of course because we'd never known one another properly I'd find it impossible to think of him as really being my father, he'd be just a man behaving the way a man ought to behave, and his wife would have been frigid or ill or something for years and years, so when we finally had the chance to be alone together chemistry would sort of take over and—"

She was flushing clear down to breast level and her free hand was hovering suggestively over her bush and her voice was becoming low and breathy. He shook free of her.

"Four minutes," he said. "And I would keep my promise to put you out in the street naked. If you'd rather go back in the gutter and stay there."

She took half a step back, clenching her fists. "You weren't like this last night!" she accused.

"You were so full of Dutch courage I don't know what you were like yesterday. Apart from stupid. And that seems to hold good for this morning as well, so—"

"You bastard!"

"Have it your way." He bent over and gathered up the foul bundle of her torn clothes and threw it at her. She made no attempt to catch it. "Put them on and get out. Or don't bother, and still get out. You've had your chance."

"You know bloody well I couldn't possibly do that!"

"Of course I do! *So why are you still pretending that you can?*"

There was a silence during which her face crumpled and she tried to find somewhere to look that wouldn't make her start crying again: the bed, the open wardrobe, the luxury suite of shower and bidet and toilet all in matching avocado porcelain with gold-plated fit-

ments, the incredible window offering its view of sub-
tropical beaches lined with palm trees and fringed with
white-foaming breakers.

Eventually, when he judged she had endured enough,
he let his voice soften.

"Poor kid," he said. "Poor silly kid. Nobody ever
made you choose for yourself before, did they?"

Dumbly she shook her head, still trying to find a
place to rest her gaze.

"It was all done for you. You didn't choose to be
raised in a one-parent family. You didn't choose to be
sent to a boarding school. You didn't really choose to
run away from it. You were driven to that, weren't
you?"

She nodded, screwing her eyes shut to prevent tears
leaking from them. She failed; they made snail tracks
down her cheeks.

"And when you did take the only big decision of
your life you discovered you had no faintest notion how
to cope with the real world. Isn't that the long and the
short of it? You thought you were going to see some
'real life' for once. You want that most of all. But you
never had the chance to learn what's real, did you? You
were brought up to mistake the fake for the genuine,
the smart for the substantial, the fashionable for the du-
rable, the impressive for the thing worth having."

She had kept her eyes shut; now she was rocking
back and forth on her heels, making every motion into
a nod that emphasized her agreement with her entire
body. Her fists were clenched before her at the level of
her waist, and her knuckles stood out pale against the
rest of her hands.

"Which is why when you meet the real you think it's
an acid flash!"

"But it can't be real!" she said doggedly, still with
her eyes closed. "I mean, a place like this in a street
like this . . . !"

"*Have* it your way. I won't stop you. Get back to
what you believe to be the real world. Pick up those
clothes and put them on!"

Spinning on his heel, he slammed shut the wardrobe door.

"No! No!" Terror rang in her voice; she raised her hands before her as to ward off a blow, and her eyes widened in the beginning of belief. Godwin noted these reactions with less than complete approval. Everything was going so fast, so predictably. There was no real challenge in his kind of work any more. If only he had been set to tackle someone relatively invulnerable . . .

But here he was, and here she was, and that was that. He was obliged to make the best of things.

Rasping: "What the hell is unreal about my home? I suppose that bed's a fake, right? You spent all night on a patch of bare boards! And it's actually freezing cold in here and you've got goose pimples all over you! And I had the Peasmarsh labels made up and paid for them to be sewn into phony clothes your size specially so when you turned up I could impress you! And you didn't drink freshly squeezed orange juice and freshly brewed Blue Mountain coffee and you didn't fill your belly with free-range eggs scrambled with Cornish butter and chopped chives and you didn't wipe your stupid arse with tissue off that roll right there!"

By now he was panting with the force of his diatribe and she was flinching and casting about as though in search of somewhere to hide.

"Ah, shit!" he exploded by way of a climax. "I thought I was doing you a favor. Most people think it's kind of a favor to be offered their heart's desire. So you're different. So you'd rather wallow in the dirt until you rot."

"No!" She clutched at him, the tears still streaming down; she was snuffling now, as her nose filled with fluid. "No, it's just that nobody ever gave me this kind of chance ever in my whole life before! I mean, you can't blame me for finding it unreal! Can you? *Can* you?"

"Ah, hell . . . I suppose not." With careful timing he put one arm around her and gave a squeeze; it coincided precisely with the next time she exhaled and obliged her to take an unusually deep breath.

"Okay, make it ten minutes instead of five. But I warn you: you've already wasted half of them, and Hermann doesn't like to be kept waiting."

Infinitely relieved, on the point of stepping under the shower at last, she hesitated.

"Who's Hermann?"

"Someone who can straighten out that mixed-up head of yours. Stop asking questions! If you can't learn to take things for granted, you won't make out in the world where I live. And you'd like that, wouldn't you?"

"You think I could?"

"That's up to you. From me you get today's help, and that is all!"

Eyes bright now, lips pressed tight together for fear of letting out something else better unsaid, she turned the shower control at random and succeeded in half scalding herself. Godwin sighed. One of these days, one of these years, maybe he'd be called to tackle some really tough assignment, or at least an assignment which would feel as tough as those he had undertaken in the past.

Maybe, though, that was inherently impossible now. Maybe he understood his techniques too well, deployed them with excessive facility . . .

No. That couldn't be the case. Surely not. So the next one, with a bit of luck, might occupy him for a reasonable length of time, give him a sense of working at full stretch, of achievement, of fulfillment. But it wasn't, of course, for him to say.

He could only hope, and hope that his hoping might be noticed.

"You'll find knickers to fit you in that drawer," he said, pointing, when Gorse emerged from the shower frantically toweling down. "Two minutes to go. You'd better hurry."

THE weather was cool today, but dry. There was, of course, a cruising taxi at the end of the street; the driver spotted Godwin's signal and waited for him. They picked their way among a horde of bored Sunday-morning children, mostly inspecting rubbish to find out whether it was salable. One of the front wheels from the Mark X Jaguar had been stolen during the night.

"Why do you live here?" Gorse demanded.

"Anywhere is as good as anywhere else," Godwin sighed, closing the door of the cab and announcing their destination. He was getting bored with her inability to see what to him was plain as pikestaffs.

At least she took the hint and held her tongue for the duration of the journey.

The taxi dropped them in the Sunday vacancy of Wimpole Street. Gray stone façades frowned down as they made their way to the house where—as reported by a discreet, well-polished brass plate—Dr. Hermann Klosterberg maintained his consultancy.

"I wish I knew why you'd brought me here," Gorse complained as she followed reluctantly in Godwin's wake.

"I already told you" was his sour reply. But his mood was already changing, precisely as he had expected, and it took no more than a glance to inform him that hers was also.

Set between ranked wrought-iron railings, the richly colored teak door opened to his touch. There was time to glimpse a high-ceilinged hallway with a fine Persian carpet on the floor and several eighteenth-century landscapes in thickly gilded frames before he ushered her into the first room on the right.

This too was high-ceilinged, but nonetheless it was dark. The walls were papered with a somber pattern; the furniture was of an old-fashioned solidity; the curtains were of dark green velvet, held back with tasseled ropes of old gold, while the carpet was of a deep wine-red and seemed to absorb not only footfalls but every sound from the outside world. There was a couch stuffed with horsehair and covered in black oilcloth over which a rug was thrown, occupying a prominent position, while the only decorations consisted in three oil paintings: portraits of Freud, Jung and Ernest Jones.

At a rolltop bureau, from which he turned in a swivel chair to greet them, they found Dr. Klosterberg himself. He was a round-headed man of medium build, his hair close-cropped and graying, wearing an unremarkable dark suit with a dark blue tie. He affected pince-nez, behind which his pale eyes gleamed. He exuded an air of grave authority. Altogether he was an archetype of the psychiatrist rôle.

Beside the couch, looking as though a four-foot fir cone had been carved out of anthracite, then flattened like a cowering hedgehog, lay Adirondinatarigo. Godwin bent to pat it on the tapered end and was rewarded by a protuberation that disconcertingly exposed a band of mucous membrane as softly glossy as the inside of a human cheek, but yellowish-green and ever so slightly luminous. The mood improved further as more pheromones escaped into the air.

Simultaneously he said, "Hermann, nice to see you again. This is Gorse. Just Gorse at the moment. She's trying to decide on a surname to go with it."

"Then she should consult Ambrose, as you and I did," Hermann murmured. "Some of his opinions may be questionable, but of his ability to sense the overtones of nomenclature there is no doubt . . . How do you do, Gorse?" he added, extending his hand with a beaming smile.

She shook with him absently, staring at the scaly black mass beside the couch. "What on earth is that?" she demanded. "I could swear I saw it move when God touched it."

"Oh, that's Canaptarosigapatruleeva," Hermann said dismissively. "No need to worry about it. Just forget it's there. For the time being, that is. Later on, you can get properly acquainted with it." He bent slightly and touched one of the thick, dull-shiny, overlapping scales; it rose a centimeter and exposed another patch of membrane, this time of a fir-tree green. "Do sit down," he added. "And what seems to be the trouble?"

The atmosphere conduced to openness. Almost before she had sunk into the chair which Hermann indicated for her, Gorse had begun to pour out her life story, far more truthfully than to Godwin last night. His back to the bureau, his elbows on the arms of his swivel chair, his fingertips arched together, Hermann listened with complete attention. All the while Potanandrusabalinicta lay immobile except for an occasional ripple of its carapace.

When the breathless recital was at an end, Hermann gave a slow nod of comprehension. It was apparent from his expression that he had grasped the essence of her problem.

"First let me assure you," he said after a pause for deliberation, "you are by no means alone. Professional ethics naturally forbid me to mention names, but I can state that friends of mine—I never use the term *patient,* for reasons I'm sure I needn't spell out to someone as perceptive as yourself—friends of mine, then, whom you would instantly recognize were it permissible for me to identify them, prominent in the theater, in music and literature, in politics and diplomacy, in commerce and so forth, have sat here in this room and described just such a constellation of perplexities. In certain cases they had been plagued with them for many years of their adult life, because what they had failed to appreciate until they were well advanced in years was the necessity of learning to yield to the impact of the collective unconscious at unpredictable intervals. Precisely because it is an unconscious, it declines to obey the dictates of clocks and calendars. That knack once acquired, however, even the regrettable aftermath of experimentation with chemical substances like the ones you have tried diminishes to insignificance. Are you familiar with the concept of the collective unconscious, by the way?" His bright, pale eyes flickered to the portrait of Jung, as though to furnish her a clue.

"I've heard of it," she said after a moment's hesitation. "Isn't it supposed to be where we get our dreams from?"

"I'm afraid that's an oversimplification," Hermann said with a thin smile. "Essentially it's a pool of shared experience—shared among all of us because we happen to be human beings—which may or may not have an 'objective' existence." The interpolated quotation marks were perfectly audible. "Almost all of us have had the experience of, for instance, entering puberty or becoming parents or confronting a rival or suffering hunger, and so on. And of course we have all had the experience of being born. Inevitably certain patterns of behavior are selected for among the countless possible patterns our cerebral neurons could create. You've heard that there are more possible neuron connections in a human brain than there would be particles in the observable universe if it were packed solid? And I'm talking about any given brain: yours, mine, Godwin's."

She gave a cautious nod. Godwin, repressing the impulse to utter a loud sigh of boredom, leaned back in his chair. It was plain that Hermann's words were sinking into her mind like ink into a dry sponge, leaving their traces everywhere. She wasn't even making a pretense of resistance.

One of these years . . .

". . . isolation from which, after so many millions of years of imprinting during the course of our evolution, can trigger an urge toward self-destruction. But you are triply fortunate."

Godwin returned to full attention. Gorse was leaning forward on her chair, eyes bright and fixed on Hermann, lips a little open, hands almost curled into fists but not quite. Every few seconds she gave a vigorous nod.

"*Imprimis*," Hermann said, raising his forefinger, "you are still youthful. Learning the gift of yielding to the collective unconscious becomes more and more difficult as adult behavior patterns—some, indeed most, badly matched to reality—become rigidified in the mind. *Secundo*, you had the luck to fall in with Godwin, who is one of my oldest friends . . . not, you understand, that one believes in 'luck' as an objective phenomenon, but sometimes the poetic imagery afforded us by superstition lends a little color to the nakedly scientific landscape of one's existence. And *tertio*, Godwin had the good sense to bring you here straight away."

Apticaranogapetulami stirred and readjusted the pattern of its scales by a few millimeters here and there.

"So let us recapitulate. You would like to live the way Godwin lives, or I do, or our various friends. You would like to achieve this goal by succeeding as a designer. You believe you have the talent. You would rather begin today than at some arbitrary date in the future set for you by someone else, regardless of who that someone else might be. You feel you have been handicapped in your laudable ambitions by unwarranted interference, although you accept that some of that interference is internal, the consequence of an unwise adventure which 'seemed like a good idea at the time.' I stand ready to be corrected if I have misrepresented you."

Seeming awed by the conciseness with which she had been summed up in a handful of words, Gorse gave a firm nod.

"You're right. You're absolutely right."

"Well, that's easy, then. Lean over Coparatuleemicabicani and take a deep breath." He pointed. Confused, she turned to follow his gesture. The anthracite scales had risen so that they stood away from the supporting muscles at almost a right angle, and the membranes thereby revealed were pulsing and oozing drops of liquid. There was an acid greenish glow.

Drawn like a needle to a magnet, Gorse leaned forward and inhaled a perfume only she could detect.

Waiting for her to recover consciousness, Godwin felt a pang of irrational envy. Maybe he ought to come back to see Hermann some time. Of course he would if he must. But maybe it would be a good idea if he did it without having to.

The question hovered in his mind for a long while, unanswerable. He had spent too long doing what he must to be able to judge the rights and wrongs of doing what he felt like doing. For that, there was a proper time, and it wasn't now.

He dismissed the whole matter as Hermann inquired affably, "And how about yourself, God? I see you fresh from Irma's mill, or I'm much mistaken. *Mens sana in corpore sano*, hey?" He risked a playful jab in Godwin's ribs.

Beside the couch, which had the potency of an established symbol and therefore was of use solely for the mundane clientèle which could not possibly afford Hermann even if they were platinum-disc pop stars and therefore received ordinary therapy from him (the world he inhabited was full of "therefores," as though it made sense), Apitaculabricomulapariti folded its scales and resumed a condition of inertness. Gorse awakened.

"I needed it. I'd been called," Godwin muttered, and at the very edge of his consciousness there fluttered the hope-cum-suspicion that this statement might elicit sympathy. He was horrified inasmuch as that was possible, and repressed it.

"One should never resist the tug of the collective unconscious," Hermann said smoothly. "That way lie all sorts of psychosomatic unpleasantnesses. How are you feeling, Gorse?"

"As though I'd sprained my mind," she said around a yawn. "Golly, I don't think I ever took in so much data at one go before."

"Nor will you ever need to again. God! Take this young lady and feed her somewhere, and let her relax. That's a prescription."

"We're going to Hugo & Diana's."

"Ideal. Have a good time. Good morning!"

There was a pause. Lurabanguliticapulanduri remained as motionless as though it were carved in ebony. At last Gorse said with great timidity, "I don't quite know how to meet your fee, doctor."

"Hm?" Hermann, having nodded and smiled at them, had turned back to the bureau, where something seemingly occupied his attention. He glanced over his shoulder at her words.

"Your—your fee!"

"My dear young lady!"—removing and rapidly polishing and replacing his pince-nez—"Absultarimanipicoloto must have let me down for once! Of course, it is difficult for it to comprehend such peculiarly human notions as 'money' and 'finances,' but even so . . . !" He accorded the creature a disdainful look, designed to establish his own ultimate superiority in the context of this consulting room. "It should have dawned on you by now that everything is already paid for."

"Everything?"—in a whisper.

"Everything!"

Godwin had risen to his feet, eager to get shut of this dull-witted, self-destructive little twat. At the back of his mind he knew his mood was once more due to the presence of Catapulibampulicarato, which grew easily bored, but there was no help for that. So did he.

"You only need to know the right way to ask for it," he declared. Hermann raised one eyebrow and nodded reluctant approval.

"Our long acquaintance has borne fruit, after its fashion," he said as he rose from his chair, hand outstretched. "Now you do as I said, and all will be well. Good morning, Gorse! And remember that you now know how and when to yield to an impulse surging up from the collective unconscious. Never resist it, and you will reap a rich reward! Good morning to you also, God; let's hope it won't be long until we meet again."

On the way to the door Gorse paused and tried to imitate Godwin's gesture on arrival. But Abutaralingo-togulisica lay as unresponsive as a bone.

HUGO & Diana was having brunch in the gravity-free patio and it was beautiful: clear blue skies with just a touch here and there of puffy white cloud; inflata-couches drifting up and down in response to the breezes which a mere gesture could create in the pure, delicately scented air; long, graceful bluish-green creepers with deep red leaves arcing across the whole of the volume and bearing on their spurs dispensers of toasted crumpets awash in melted butter, Patum Peperium, smoked oysters, bitter-orange marmalade, hot coffee and hot milk, and also pitchers of buck's fizz and bloody mary. In such a flawless environment clothes seemed superfluous. Immediately on their arrival Hugo & Diana gave a cry of delight from where she lay on a long yellow couch and invited them to join him in a state of nature. Prepared for this, Godwin complied with a sigh, helped himself to a mugful of bloody mary, and cast himself adrift in the sky on a passing infla-tabed, one striped in orange and white. Gorse hesitated for a few seconds, but shortly shame got the better of her and she discarded her clothes, which gyrated around her for a while in a mocking pattern, and attempted to imitate her companions' nonchalance. Her choice of inflatabed was polka-dotted red on yellow. It took her a while to get the better of it, while Hugo & Diana bestowed indulgent glances, but very shortly she was able to draw a mug of buck's fizz—mistaking it for orange juice—and paddle her way to where Godwin was.

After necessary introductions, what she said first was "Where are we?"

"About three hundred meters from the King's Road, Chelsea," was the reply.

"I thought I knew . . ." The words died away. Godwin and Hugo & Diana exchanged amused glances. It was always like this.

So always, it would certainly cease to be amusing sooner or later.

However . . .

"You're exquisite!" caroled Hugo & Diana, expertly paddling toward Gorse. "You're a designer, is that right?"

Lost for a cue, Gorse glanced at Godwin, but he was lying back to enjoy the sunshine. She had to find her own way through this one.

"Yes," she said boastfully, and gulped down the contents of her glass. "And so are you! Everybody knows the Peasmarsh label now. Those things I just took off—" She gestured as the liquor began to affect her.

"What do you want?" Companionably, Hugo & Diana linked her inflatabed to hers. "Start with basics. Underwear? Tights? Shoes? Slippers? Shirts and blouses? Skirts and trousers? Short dresses and long ones? Coats and capes and cloaks? Hats, handbags, bracelets, necklaces, watches, rings, handkerchiefs, scarves, combs and hairbrushes and toothbrushes, soap and toothpaste, cologne and deodorant, face powder and lipsticks, eye shadow and mascara, assorted perfumes, nail files and scissors, emery boards, nail varnish and cuticle removers, shampoo and conditioner, bath salts and bath oil, sponges and loofahs, soap and cleansing cream and depilatory and tweezers and shavers and hair driers and sun-ray lamps and sun-screen lotions and swimsuits and bikinis and trikinis and bathing caps and sandals and toweling robes and glasses and sunglasses and boots and breeches and gloves and your choice of sanitary towels or the means to render them permanently unnecessary and that ought to do for the present. Will it?" He smiled dazzlingly. "We aim to offer a complete service, but you may have thought of something I left out. Naturally everything will bear the Peasmarsh label unless you'd rather it was marked Quant or Dior or whatever. Up to you."

By this time she had insinuated himself on to the same inflatabed as Gorse and cast the other into the void.

In a softer tone he added, "Don't worry about offending me if you say you'd rather it was Dior. I think you're gorgeous anyhow, and I'm so glad God thought of bringing you to us. But then, of course, he does have *taste*, doesn't he? And anybody with taste can get on in the world. It's just about the rarest thing on earth, and if you have it, it's like a magic touchstone— Did you know we're into magic? Oh, you must have realized! Of course it does require a terrific investment of psychical energy, but we are exceptionally well endowed. Now and then it leads to a period of inescapable replenishment, but even computers have to have their downtime, don't they?"

By this time she was fondling Gorse's clitoris and his prick was standing to attention. Godwin, trying hard not to yawn, helped himself to more of the bloody mary. It was made with wodka Zubrowskar, and deliciously aromatic. It sufficed to pass the time until Hugo & Diana had finished and Gorse was cast away again on another of the countless floating couches.

"So"—with sudden businesslike briskness— "that lot would suit you? We'll arrange for it to be delivered. God, where are you stashing her? Bill's, as usual?"

Godwin risked shrugging, even though it made his own couch bob around violently in midair.

"Where else?"

"Fine! And I promise you"—this to Gorse, across the intervening void—"you not only won't but you can't regret deciding to have the Peasmarsh label on everything. There are certain principles transcending science which led us to design our trademark, and they resonate from anything it's printed on or even attached to. If you have even a trace of doubt concerning what we're saying, look around you. *Si evidentiam requiris, circumspice!*"

"You mean," she responded in a voice full of excitement, "I could have a place like this?" She gazed about her; there were marble statues, floating flags of every conceivable color, water sculptures which maintained their unnervingly accurate course against all odds. Godwin had seen it so often, he was bored, though he did wish he could share her impressionability.

"No, no!" exclaimed Hugo & Diana in dismay. "Not at all like this! This is mine! But you can certainly have what *you* want. Think it over. Make up your mind in due time. When you do, we promise I'll come and see it."

In a lower, more confidential tone, she added, "But you must be sure to incorporate the power signs which act as channels for the magic. We've been telling God that for—oh, ages and ages! And do you think we can get him to pay attention? Not on your what's-it! But never mind"—with a sudden renewal of brilliant charm. "You do it the way you want, and have your kind of fun."

Godwin, relieved at the chance to leave, signaled Gorse to rejoin him. She came slowly, relishing the weird sensation of floating, and as she arrived within range of his hand, which she caught at, she said, "Is it magic that pays for . . . ? Well, for all of this?"

"Well, we don't," Hugo & Diana said, turning her back and pushing off into the empyrean and beginning to caress his clitoris with sighs and moans of pleasure. "Who could? Nobody could! It isn't to be bought, is it?"

"But if—" Gorse ventured obstinately. Godwin cut her short with a gesture and handed her the clothes she had been wearing when they got here. He noticed that as she donned each separate garment she looked at the Peasmarsh label in search of the magical symbols she had just been told about.

Well, one couldn't expect everybody to grow up at once.

"Let's go," he said finally, and led the way to the street. This being Sunday, and in Chelsea, poor weather had not prevented crowds of people from assembling in order to surge back and forth in aimless droves.

As they walked toward where Godwin knew a taxi would—of course—be cruising empty, Gorse's face grew paler and paler.

"I never did anything so awful in my life!" she burst out at last.

"What do you mean?"

"You know damned well!" She bit her lip as though to keep tears away. "I don't know what came over me!"

"Not to worry," Godwin sighed. "Hugo & Diana has that effect on people. It's part of the package. Done with what they call pheromones, I gather."

"But what sort of a creature is—is it?"

"Hermaphrodite, of course. Maybe one of these days you'll meet the surgeon who performed the transplants. Brilliant man."

"Are you taking me to meet another monster now?"

There was the taxi; Godwin hailed it, and resumed when they were inside.

"We're going to see Ambrose Farr."

"And what's he going to make me do that I don't want to?"

"If you hadn't wanted to do what you did, you wouldn't have done it."

"But I didn't!"

Typical. Typical! Godwin sighed, doing his best to repress an outbreak of bad temper.

"You want a name to go with Gorse. Ambrose is good at choosing names. He'll pick one for you."

"And if I don't like it?"

"You will."

The mechanics went on, like cogwheels inexorably turning.

"He will also do a great deal more than pick a name."

"Such as what?"

"Tell you who you are, and who you would be better off being."

"But I know who I am!"

"You may think you do. Ambrose will tell you if you're right."

"And if he thinks I'm wrong?"—resentfully.

"He'll tell you that, too. Make for Putney, driver! I'll direct you when we get close."

IMPROBABLY interpolated among tall modern buildings: a cottage with its garden running down to a towpath alongside the Thames. There was an iron gate, waist-high, set in the fence which bordered tidy twin strips of bright green lawn converging on the white façade under the red-tiled roof. Small round flower beds isolated clumps of tulips, hollyhocks and poppies. Creepers disposed with flawless symmetry ornamented the front wall's edges to left and right.

Someone lived here who cared about minutiae.

But at a second glance there were reasons why the prospect should be as it was.

There were adequately few people who understood what kind of a glance they should give it the second time.

Accordingly there was nobody who paid attention when Godwin marched Gorse up the path to the bright yellow front door.

Except, naturally, the occupier.

The door opened as usual to Godwin's touch and revealed a narrow hallway with a flagged floor. The flags, each a meter square, numbered twelve, and each bore a zodiacal sign, inlaid yellow on a deep red ground. The walls were divided into panels with dark brown wooden moldings; each panel displayed a card from the Bembo version of the tarot pack, including the otherwise lost *The Devil* and *The Tower*. Heady and intoxicating incense loaded the air with dense masses of perfume. Solemn organ music resounded at the edge of hearing.

At the far end of the hallway a doorway flickered open and shut, and a fraction later another to the left: the former uttered, the latter received, a tall fair graceful boy clad only in a white shirt.

Godwin halted on the flag displaying Libra. Following him, nervous, Gorse found herself on the one signing Virgo, just as there came a subtle increase in volume of the background music; also there was a change of register, so that a series of bright and lively phrases, mostly in triplets, overran the ground chords with a sparkling rivulet of treble tones.

And there was their host: a tall man wearing a dark brown velvet suit which somehow contrived to give the impression of robes, even though it was splendidly cut to fit. At his throat was a lace jabot, and a white silk handkerchief cascaded from his breast pocket. He bore himself with the commanding air of full maturity, but it was impossible to judge his age, for his skin—which was smoothly tanned—was wrinkle-free except around the eyes, where one might detect laughter lines, and contrasting with his tan he had a leonine mane of swept-back hair which might, or might not, have been white rather than ash-blond. His voice was of a thrilling deepness, yet every now and then it turned up at the corners, so to say, as though a sternly engraved face on a statue were occasionally unable to resist hinting at a smile, and nearly but never completely implied a giggle.

"My dear fellow!" he boomed as he advanced, both hands outstretched to clasp Godwin's right hand and his elbow in a single gesture. "It's been too long—it always is too long! And who's your . . . charming young friend?"

There was a significance about the pause. But that was to be expected. Godwin gave a bald answer.

"This is Ambrose Farr," he said, turning. "Ambrose, this is Gorse. Just Gorse, at the moment."

"Delighted to make your acquaintance!" Ambrose declared warmly, extending his right arm at full stretch and abbreviating contact with Gorse's hand to a minimum. For the obviousness of this he was at once apologetic.

"You'll forgive me! But I carry a certain astral charge which is at risk of diminishment—not, of course, that one would suspect such a risk in the case of someone brought here by an old and good friend like him!"

The not-quite-giggle added a string of extra exclamation marks to his statement. A heartbeat later, though, he was intensely businesslike in both tone and manner.

"How wise of you, at all events, to consult an expert in nomenclature before settling on your permanent appellation. The careers, the entire lives, which I've seen ruined by an inappropriate choice . . . Perhaps you've never considered the point, though merely by looking at you I would deduce that you have, but I can state with conviction that the vibrations which resonate from names affect even such fundamental aspects of the personality as the way in which one regards oneself. How much wiser are those cultures which employ different names at different ages! How unfortunate is, let us say, a Helen who turns out to be fat and pimply rather than a queen for beauty, or a Dorothy whose parents resent her because they hoped she'd be a boy! Your selection, though, is Gorse: a prickly plant, with certain medicinal virtues, which in summer is capable of transforming mile upon square mile of landscape into a wonderland of brilliant yellow—already an inspiration. With overtones, regrettably, of deception and entrapment . . . Hmm! God, you have brought me a problem worthy of my steel. We shall devote entire attention to it, never fear. Come down into my sanctum that we may perform analyses."

He was standing, so it seemed, stock-still in the middle of the passageway. Nonetheless, as though responsive to his mere intention, two of the tarot-painted panels folded back: *The Juggler* and *The Fool*. Between them appeared the head of a stairway leading down to a dim-lit basement. A few wreaths of smoke wafted forth.

"I must precede you," he murmured, doing so. "There are certain barriers and rituals . . ."

Producing—from his sleeve, or somewhere—an ebony wand capped at one end with silver, at the other with ivory, he descended the stairs, making signs at intervals. Gorse, biting her thumb, hung back, her eyes immensely wide. There seemed to be no limit to the depth the staircase reached.

Losing patience, Godwin took her by the left arm and urged her ahead of him, and a few seconds later they were in what Ambrose referred to as his sanctum.

It gave the appearance, once they were within it, of having neither roof nor walls: only a floor of cold irregular stone. At one place glowed a brazier on which reposed an alembic distilling a luminous fluid; at another, two human skeletons, male and female, were mounted to suggest that they were about to grapple, wrestler-fashion; elsewhere, floating in midair, hung a stuffed crocodile and a dried bat; beyond that, at first, there appeared to be no more than banks of fog.

Then Ambrose turned on a light, and the illusion vanished. Instead of misty obstacles to vision, it was plain that the boundaries of the place were formed by ranks and layers of charts drawn on two-meter-square sheets of some transparent substance, which rustled at the slightest draft like dead leaves. Each consisted in a series of circles, sometimes concentric, sometimes overlapping, sometimes of alarming complexity and number, crossed with straight lines and marked with symbols in contrasting colors, mostly letters of the Greek and Hebrew alphabets but in some cases quite unfamiliar.

But these were not the most astonishing feature of the place once it was possible to see it clearly.

Ambrose had sat down in a slingback canvas chair beside a foursquare teak desk which might have come directly out of the headquarters of a multinational corporation anxious to maintain its executives' illusions concerning their current status, on which was mounted an elaborate computer complex including a full-scale word-processing setup. One of the screens was visible from where Gorse and Godwin stood, and it was cycling a dozen rings of different colors around a central dot.

Catching sight of it, Ambrose muttered an oath and hit a switch, then beamed falsely at his visitors.

"*So* sorry! But they're talking about a certain Royal Personage getting married, so I thought I'd just run through a few alternative sequences, but naturally, once one gets to *that* level, the interplay of conflicting possibilities attains *alarming* proportions, so I simply let it run, and . . ." A shrug. Then a winning smile. "You will forget you ever saw it, won't you? Yes? Bless you. And, speaking of attaining alarming proportions, just let me tell Anders what I'm up to . . . *Do* sit down!"

There were comfortable chairs for them, which they did not remember from a moment ago. It was all part of the scenario, but Gorse was trembling worse than ever as she lowered herself into hers. Meantime, Ambrose whispered to an invisible microphone. Then he was paying attention to them again, this time addressing Gorse directly.

"I sense you have a question, young lady. May I answer it?"

She swallowed hard, indicating the panels all about them. "What are these?"

"What do you think they might be?" he countered with an affably avuncular air.

"Uh . . . Well, they make me think of horoscope charts, but—"

"God, you briefed her in advance!" Ambrose interrupted accusingly.

Godwin sighed, leaned back, shook his head, feigned a smile.

"In that case I'm impressed," Ambrose said, leaning forward and interlinking his fingers. He had contrived to make his wand disappear without trace. "These are, let's face it, a trifle more *explicit* than most such charts. For instance, I had been prepared for some few weeks to see God again, thanks to his." He sig-

naled, and a chart presented itself as though they were
all on an automatic retrieval system—and instantly he
snapped his fingers and it vanished again into the con-
tinually circulating background, while he bent a white-
toothed smile on Godwin.

"*You* know I would never show anybody your chart
without your permission, save for such a fleeting instant . . . and that only because I am of course proud
that I am privy to it! And, as I was about to say, even
the most advanced of my—ah—fellow adepts would
have trouble unraveling the coding it bears, because I
take into account the totality of variables." He patted the
case of his word processor. "For instance, I imagine no
one, even Della, drawing on the fullness of the oriental
tradition, could match this"—once more, a chart
floated into view and paused, and displayed a set of
interlocking ring patterns so complicated they required
color separations at the limit of human discrimina-
tion—"which I cast for a certain world-famous figure,
who turned out to be remarkably keenly influenced by
the lately discovered moon of Pluto. There is, however,
a beat frequency which I suspect may be due to interference from the asteroidal belt, given that this induces
a type of static, or background noise, owing to the sheer
randomness of the interactions—except that actually, of
course, it's *non*random, insofar as while the micro-
cosmic world may be subject to the laws of chance, the
macrocosmic isn't— Ah, but I tend to ramble when I
get away on my hobbyhorse. At least, though, I might
be permitted to show you this, for an example of how I
find myself obliged to seek distraction when the de-
mands of my profession grow extreme . . . which, I
must admit, they tend to do with gratifying frequency
nowadays, since I am constantly being consulted by
cabinet ministers and diplomats and the like, or their
wives—nowadays I must surely say 'spouses'—and
their children, if that case applies, ha-hah! But at all
events, I suspect you may not recognize *this*."

A chart appeared whose central element resembled
the symbol for infinity: ∞ . In red and yellow it

gleamed from the middle of a series of tidily patterned elliptical rings, all of them far from the two which interlocked at the focus.

These were green, yellow, reddish-brown and white.

All the time he had been talking, music had continued; now it climaxed on a resounding chord of trumpets and trombones, and died away like a gasp.

"No?" And without waiting for an answer: "I'm not surprised. This is the generalized chart for a species whose home planet orbits a double star in Cassiopeia, and they're like oysters or maybe snails because they're intermittently bisexual and— What *am* I thinking of? I meant to ask your data so the computer could chew them over for a while. I had a new chart all prepared because from God's I knew he was about due to bring me someone complicated—won't bother to demonstrate, but . . ." Now he was muttering and a plain chart was hovering before him.

"Birth date, please. Time of day if you know it. Whatever you can tell me about your parents' sexual habits—whether they fucked on weekends only or whether your father had to force your mother or whether he was more potent in the morning or at night or whether she felt more like it at certain phases of her menstrual cycle or *anything*. It'll all go in here." He swiveled to face the computer keyboard. "Because time of conception is also very useful in figuring out the astral forces which would have obtained."

Godwin, who had been through all this much too often, leaned back and disconnected. At some point Anders kissed him hello, but he wasn't in the mood, or any mood.

At long last Ambrose was saying, "*Well?*"

"I'm not sure I like it," Gorse answered doubtfully.

"You don't believe that a name resonates and creates beat frequencies with the astral forces working on a person?" Ambrose demanded. "I'll prove it if you like! Here, where's the chart for that one? When the Duchess of Anglia had her second son—the one born after the duke died—they baptized him with the same name as his father, stupid *gits*. If only they'd bothered to consult me . . . !"

Appealing, Gorse turned her eyes to Godwin, who summoned his remaining forces and donned a smile.

"What did you suggest?" he said in a conciliating tone.

"He wants to call me Gorse Plenty!" Gorse said before Ambrose could rush to his own defense. "And it's not a name I ever heard of and I don't like it anyway!"

"It's right for you! It's perfect!" Ambrose barked. He was on his feet by now, grossly offended.

"It was Ambrose who gave me my name," Godwin said placatingly, also rising. "And I've never regretted taking his advice."

"Precisely, and thank you! Any more than Cineraria Howe regretted it—and doesn't everybody know her name from the television series she's been in? As for County Barbarian, if it weren't for me, even his gimmick of being a millionaire's son wouldn't have got his bunch of second-rate slags into the Top Twenty with the sort of material they were using! And I could multiply this list *indefinitely*! Didn't you know CB's original name was Edgar Bernard Brown? Heaven help us! If I wanted to write a five-syllable curse, I'd be hard put to it to improve on that one!"

"Curse?" Gorse parried faintly.

"What else do you call it when your initials spell 'ebb'? That's a *downer*—as my contacts among the youth generation inform me." This with a sudden shy, almost boyish smile. "But you've struck lucky, I promise. Your friends at school must have had a clearer overall perception of your potential than you did yourself, let alone the teachers—or so-called teachers—you were forced to suffer under. As for your mother . . . !" This ended in an elaborate shudder. "Nonetheless, a counteragent to the harshness of the name you enjoy wearing will stand you in good stead in the long run. Apart from anything else, it will be memorable, and all the people who bear interchangeable names will envy you. *True?*"

"Ambrose bestows good names," Godwin said hastily. "His is the other name of Merlin, the magician."

"Right!" Ambrose crowed, clapping Godwin on the shoulder. "So when I say 'Plenty' is correct, you must remember: 'Gorse' is a sparse, repugnant plant, symbolic of deprivation. You want that? Of course not!"

He switched out lights without moving, and all of a sudden the sanctum was dank and unbearable. Gorse moved toward where the stairs had been, her teeth audibly chattering.

"*This* way," Ambrose murmured. "We shall drink a glass of firewine to your acceptable appellation."

And indeed the steps were yards away, beyond the dried bat and immediately below. The stove had brewed its ichor and the alembic was dull gray; the odor of incense had given way to something vaguely putrid, as of cow-guts cast aside by a butcher, and overlooked.

In a gracious room above Anders made them welcome, clad now in blue jeans and rope-soled sandals. From a crystal decanter he poured into crystal glasses four measures of something which fumed and glowed, neither red nor green but partway between.

Ambrose gave a formal toast.

"Long may it, soon may it, and may we live to enjoy it!"

They drank in unison. Gorse had meant to sip, not gulp, but Anders was well trained—as Ragnar had been, and Per and Horst and Lars and all those others who bore *echt*-Aryan cognomens—and at precisely the right moment he contrived to jog her elbow and she swallowed the lot, even as Ambrose was stating didactically, "This so-called firewine is of course no more than a distillate of certain significant herbs whose governing planets relate to the subject, but you would have to travel far—you note *my* name, Farr?—before you

found a match as regards appropriateness for this particular brew. Young lady, I wish you vast success from
your identity, but I must withdraw because tomorrow I
am to be consulted by an official of the United Nations
whose wife disapproves—stupid bitch!—of his interest
in my work, and to be absolutely and utterly frank,
your mere presence as a *female* distorts the aura I am
attempting to create in this house. Honestly, God, can
you not choose your times better?"

That was so absurd, ridiculous, and pointless a question, Godwin was shaken by it. He thought for a while,
and at last ventured, "You mean Anders is nursing a
hard-on."

"If his psychic energy were to be wasted on the air—!"
protested Ambrose, making a gesture to encompass
the collapse of universes.

"I don't choose my times," Godwin said, and set
his glass on the nearest table. "Gorse didn't choose.
Think about it. Thanks for the wine. But I think 'Gorse
Plenty' will work out fine.

"In case you were still worried."

There was a long pause during which Anders
shrugged and turned to leave. Ambrose checked him
with an affectionate arm linked about his neck.

"What now, God? I promise, I *am* interested. But for
the fact which you know about. I wish Aleister were
here to speak on my behalf."

"You always wish that. It's your way . . . But FYI:
there are material considerations. Come on, Gorse, let's
get out of here. You haven't even met Bill yet, and you
must. After all, he's going to be your landlord."

IN the taxi which naturally they picked up within a few yards of Ambrose's door she said to him fretfully, "I don't understand."

"That doesn't surprise me."

"But I don't!"—in a near wail. "You seem to know all these people, but who are they?"

"People I've known for a long time."

"Oh, *for God's sake!*" She hunched away from him. "What are you all? Some kind of group?"

"Yes, in a sense, I suppose."

"Like the Rosicrucians?"

Godwin stifled a laugh. In his gravest tone he said, "No, not in the least."

"Well, then . . ." She was biting her lower lip so hard it might bleed. "I wish I understood what was going on!"

"You only need to understand the consequences."

"All the time you say things like that! This guy— what's his name?—this Ambrose: he was full of double-talk, wasn't he?"

"You don't have to take Ambrose too seriously."

"But a while ago you were saying I must!" She turned to him with her large eyes full of tears. "Or is it that you're trying to brainwash me?"

"Brainwashing is done by deprivation and lack of sleep and repetition of some kind of ideological message until the defences of the mind give way under the overload. They used it in Korean prisoner-of-war camps. They use it nowadays in Ulster police stations. The essential element is monotony. What, *pray,* is either monotonous or even predictable about what we've been doing? And I can testify that when I got through with you last night, you enjoyed several hours' deep sleep. Did you know you snore?"

"I don't!"

"Oh yes you do. Not very loudly, but with a kind of bubbly noise. You probably have a post-nasal drip that needs attention."

"You're trying to make me follow a red herring! That isn't what I'm talking about! I've read *The Golden Ass*, you know. A certain kind of shock can be just as efficacious as a prolonged period of deprivation in converting someone, and that's what you're trying to do, isn't it? You're trying to convert me to some sort of belief which— Golly! Excuse me!" Her words were dissolving into a colossal yawn.

This soon? Even before arriving at Bill's place? Well, perhaps it was all for the best. Godwin had no faintest notion what she was going on about, but he had spinal tremors which indicated bad news, and while it was un-precedented for the owners to be in such a hurry, it might well be for the best if she underwent a chastening experience right away. At least it would be better from his point of view than suffering through the usual load of crap—"Oh, all my life I've dreamed of guid-ance from on high!" or "Isn't it fantastic to think that someone actually *understands* and can *put to use* the astral forces which surround us?" or, perhaps worst of the lot, "Doesn't it just *prove* that when it's properly attuned the miracle which is the human mind is capable of concretizing anything our imagination has ever con-ceived of?"

But all this making with the mouth was boring his balls off, and he earnestly looked forward to dumping Gorse and getting on with something he cared about. However, by this time she was not only yawning, but threatening to doze off, and with all possible respect to whoever was calling her, he had no wish to carry her bodily into the house when they reached their destina-tion. So he talked rapidly and loudly.

"I think you'll get on well with Bill Harvey—your

temporary landlord, you know, the guy whose house you're going to live in until you find your feet and get a place of your own. An interesting bloke. Used to be a jockey, and then a flyweight boxer, and still has the broken nose to prove it. A bit like dueling scars in his circle, having a broken nose. I remember he once told me that when he was a kid the big man in his personal world was the landlord, whose agent kept coming around to dun his mother for the rent, so he decided one day he was going to be a landlord himself, and now he owns houses all over South London—Catford, Lee Green, New Cross, Peckham . . . He prides himself on being a good landlord; he swears he never hires any-one to do anything he can't do himself, from painting and rewiring down to drains and concrete floors."

Was he going to have to go on and talk about Bill's one visible shortcoming? Gorse's head was nodding and her eyelids kept drifting down, but—thank good-ness—they were now rounding the corner of the street where Bill lived. Godwin thrust a fiver at the cabby and told him to keep the change, and just as he opened the door Bill appeared to lend him a hand.

"She looks as if she's being called already!" he whis-pered as he caught the drowsy girl under the arms with all the expertise due to helping fellow boxers away from the ring after a catastrophic defeat.

"Yes, I think so. Better get her inside as fast as possi-ble," Godwin answered.

But Gorse was able to stand and walk by herself as she was led into the house, even though she kept cast-ing glances to either side, for this was a decaying street, down on its luck, and the frontages and roofs were even more in need of repair than those where Godwin lived, while the curbs were lined with abandoned cars, some of which had been set on fire and burned to discolored metal skeletons.

"I have to live here?" she said in faint horror.

"You won't find a better 'ouse in London that takes in lodgers on the spur of the moment," Bill declared. "Not since the Rent Acts you won't!"

He was a remarkable figure, and people were looking at him from across the street as hard as Gorse was staring at his disreputable-seeming home, with its unpainted woodwork and rusty guttering, all in accordance with his ingrained principle that one should do nothing to attract the attention of the tax collectors. He affected clothing that two or three generations ago would have been considered flash: a brown check suit with brilliantly polished brown boots, a yellow shirt, a green silk tie with a pearl sticker in it, and—even for this brief excursion into the open air—the same brown bowler hat he would have worn on a trip to Epsom for the Derby.

"All the gear you're getting from Hugo & Diana is being sent here," Godwin improvised. "And remember, this is only temporary—*and* of course once you're settled in, you'll find it's much nicer than it looks from the outside. Remember how you felt about my place!"

Had she not been so sleepy by now, though, it was plain she would have resisted their attempts to steer her along the hallway and into a room on the right. From the rear of the house came faint noises: a running commentary on a horse race, growing momently more frenzied.

"I picked Shahanshah yesterday at twenty to one—did you 'ave anything on 'im?" Bill inquired as he opened the door of the room so that Godwin could steer Gorse through it. By now she was again stumbling with her eyes shut, fighting and failing to stay awake. The room had been repapered with a hideous design of huge orange and pink roses on a sky-blue ground, but otherwise it was precisely as Godwin remembered: the narrow bed, the second-hand armchair, the rickety table and upright chair, the curtained alcove in the corner for hanging clothes, the chest of drawers with a mismatched handle on the left of the bottom drawer, the washbasin with the exposed plumbing, the electric shower in a tin cabinet with a torn plastic curtain across the front, even the battered tin wastebasket with a design of daffodils.

Of course, it wasn't yet activated. It would take a while for Gorse to learn how to do that, but she would. And then it might well be quite some time before she decided to move elsewhere.

They laid her on the bed and within seconds she had rolled on one side and begun to utter that trace of a snore which Godwin had rebuked her for: a tiny bubbling sound on every intake of breath, and a pop-and-wheeze on every exhalation. Nervously Bill said, "I think we better get out of 'ere and shut the door, don't you?"

"Yes. She's very close. I wouldn't put it more than half an hour away."

They retreated to the hallway, where Bill retrieved a tankard half full of bitter which he had left on an occasional table. Raising it significantly, he said, "Want to pop in the parlor for a minute, sink a jar? I missed the end of the race but I can rerun it. After that I got a terrific cup-tie—everybody said Rovers 'ad it made, but I said United and I was right! Even though that was before I got my new amulet. You know what an amulet is? Truly? Ah, might've known you'd 'ave 'eard of 'em before. Smart aleck! Puts all my other gear in the shade, though. Swear it does!"

He made an all-encompassing gesture. On the occasional table stood a vase; it contained white heather. Over the front door a horseshoe was nailed, open end down; Godwin recalled what agonies Bill had been through, wondering which view was correct—whether if it were upside down all the luck would run out, or whether it should be mounted so that luck would fall on those who passed beneath. The latter had prevailed, but he had one the other way up at the back door, just in case. It was his conviction that charms and cantrips had brought him his good fortune, and he had made his home into a kind of museum of superstitions.

Wearily and not without malice Godwin said, "Did you have anything on Shahanshah?"

"Me? Not bleedin' likely! Won't let me in the bettin' shop any more, the buggers won't! Won't let me do the

pools neither! Just 'cause all the time I'm right an'
they're wrong! But you're 'avin' me on, aren't you? I
could swear I told you what they done to me down the
bettin' shop!"

"Maybe you ought to turn in your amulets and try
your luck all by yourself for a change," Godwin suggested dryly.

"Thought of that," Bill answered with a lugubrious
scowl. "But the way I look at it, you're better off bein'
lucky than unlucky, right?"

"Right."

"Sure you won't stop off for a jar?" Bill went on,
having drained his tankard. "I got the place done over
real nice now. You couldn't tell it from Frinton-on-Sea,
I'd take my oath on that. And I got barrels and barrels
of beer—lager, bitter, stout, whatever you fancy!"

Godwin was spared the need to refuse by a sudden
racket emanating from Gorse's room: great clumsy
stamping sounds, then the noise of something being
knocked over—probably the chair—and curses in a
deep, unfeminine voice.

"Either come on in, or scarper toot sweet!" Bill
whispered. "I never fancy meetin' any of me lodgers
when they're—well, *you* know!"

Nodding, Godwin repressed a shudder. Indeed, it
must be eerie to meet a stranger in a familiar body.

Something tinny: the wastebasket being kicked or
hurled at the wall.

"Gawblimey, I'll 'ave to paper the room *again* . . .
Well?"

"I'm going to scarper. Sorry. Next time with luck.
You fix the luck, okay?"

"Okay."

But it was a sickly grin he gave Godwin as he shook
hands and he couldn't refrain from glancing at the door
of the room to see whether it was bulging yet under an
attack from the other side. Often it took quite some
while for the owner to get adjusted.

"Funny . . ." Bill said as he turned away. He spoke

in a musing tone. "Sometimes I'd give anything . . . You been called lately, 'ave you?"

"What do you think I'm doing here?" And, impelled by the same need which had caused him to speak up at Irma's, and knowing what he had to say would register on Bill if anyone, he suddenly produced from his pocket the press cutting which included him in a list of heroes decorated at Buckingham Palace. "I got the George Medal for it," he muttered. "See?"

"Crikey!" Bill said, his eyes widening. "The George Medal, eh? Wish I 'ad 'arf your imagination! I thought I was pitchin' it a bit strong when I backed Lovely Cottage for the National!"

He studied the press cutting avidly. But before he could make a further comment, they were interrupted by a real crash from Gorse's room: probably the hand-basin shattering. Godwin hastily retrieved the slip of paper and made for the door.

"See yourself out!" Bill invited ironically, and turned back to the kitchen. Struck by a thought, however, he checked.

"Show me that again!"

"Uh . . . Well, if you like." Godwin complied, feeling for some unaccountable reason extremely nervous—not because of the renewed noises from the room, but because there was a frown on Bill's usually cheerful face.

"September the twentieth," Bill said at last, tapping the paper with a blunt forefinger.

"Yes!"

"1940?"

"Yes, of course—during the Blitz!"

"I don't believe it," Bill said with finality, surrendering the paper again.

"Nobody's asking you to!" Godwin snapped, returning it to his pocket. But a sour taste was gathering in his mouth, and he forced himself to add the crucial question: "Why?"

"Weren't no George Medals then, nor George Cross

neither. Didn't get introduced until September the twenty-third." Bill gave a crooked smile. "I don't waste *all* me time watchin' football on the telly. Always bin interested in the war. An' that I remember clear as daylight. September the twenty-third just 'appens to be me birthday . . . Lord, there she goes again! 'Ave that door down in a minute! Better scarper—see yer!"

A moment later Godwin was back in the dingy street under a dismal sky. People seemed to be looking at him more than even they had at Bill in his out-of-date finery. Their faces were cold and pinched with hunger. Some of the children playing in the gutter wore only ragged vests or outgrown dresses and were mechanically masturbating as they gazed at him with dull eyes.

Godwin shivered and hurried on by, pulling up the collar of his jacket against those stony, chilly stares.

But at least he could now look back on a job complete, and before claiming his reward he could afford to relax and unwind for a while. Starting today? Starting tomorrow?

There was no hurry. Sometimes there was, as though pressure were being applied, but not at present. He had time to think over what he wanted next.

And needed it. What Bill had said had disturbed him. He felt as though the foundation of his existence had been shaken, as by earthquakes.

There was only one tenable explanation. Birthday or no birthday, Bill must have made a mistake.

It was inconceivable that the owners should.

ABRUPTLY, as he was heading away from Bill's place, it dawned on Godwin that he was within easy walking distance of Harry Fenton's. On the spur of the moment he decided to go there and pick up a passport; he had used his present one twice.

But when he arrived at Harry's basement flat, in a narrow street of sleazy gray-brick houses beset—like the whole of London—with abandoned cars, there was no reply to his ring . . . this being one of the few doors which did not automatically open even to his touch.

The most likely explanation was that Harry had been called, and for that there was no help. There was never any help.

Perhaps it didn't matter. Harry's forgeries were—naturally—the finest in the world, and Godwin had not actually been warned that he shouldn't use a passport too often; it just seemed like a reasonable precaution, because there were so many countries where the police were forever demanding *"Vos papiers!"* and *"Ihr Ausweis!"*—or whatever—and the presence of a visitor unrecorded at any port or airport might entrain problems . . .

But what the hell? Shrugging, though unable to repress a scowl of annoyance, Godwin resigned himself to using the old one. He badly needed clean air and an absence of people, so there was no alternative.

As he trudged toward the nearest street where a cruising taxi could logically be intersecting with him, because it was impolitic to work even minor miracles except in carefully chosen company, his attention was caught by a little girl on the other side of the road, shaking back her fair hair. He checked in mid-stride, staring . . . and realized she could not possibly be anybody other than herself.

Thinking he might catch the last of the skiing, he made for André Bankowski's hotel at Les Hôpitaux Neufs, but even though the spring was dismal over Western Europe, the snow was already melting except on the very highest *pistes,* and the only good run he achieved was spoiled because he spotted a blond girl riding up in the *téléférique* with André while he was on the last stretch, and didn't realize until he had wandered off the line into soft crustless snow that she was too round-faced and had too large a mouth.

Compared with whose?

He sat through one boring evening in the bar and watched people getting drunk and amorous, and went to New Orleans instead, where English-born Wilfred Burgess was fulfilling his ambitions by leading a band of half-legendary jazzmen, one of whom claimed to have recorded with King Oliver. But on the corner of Bourbon and Iberville in the Vieux Carré he saw a fair-haired girl making a grand performance, for the benefit of a boyfriend, out of her attempts to eat an enormous oyster po'boy one-handed with a full but open can of beer in the other, and found himself on the point of going to her assistance before he realized she was not in fact the person he imagined.

And who was that?

Dispirited, he went to Maud McConley's in Nassau for some skin-diving, and while darting around coral reefs and enjoying his isolation and his suspension in time as well as space noticed a head of long, pale hair spread out in the water and his heart nearly stopped before he worked out that the change of color due to being under water meant that this was not the shade he had in mind.

What shade?

Alone in his magnificent hotel suite, masturbating

with desultory lack of interest, he thought the matter through and felt cheated, deceived, betrayed.

That little girl whose life he so vividly remembered saving (and to hell with Bill Harvey!): she was the key and clue. Blasé, he had grown immune to most erotic stimuli; it was the readiest form of reward someone in his position could request. But her brief kiss, so public and so shameless . . .

Merely recalling it made him climax, and the pang of that was promptly followed by disgust. He kept thinking of a single word: *pervert*.

And went back to England to find a cloudy, hesitant summer as ill-defined as his own state of mind. He half wished he might be called again, but he had not yet claimed his reward for the last time, and so far he had not thought of anything fresh he wanted to experience.

Besides, the occasions for being called were apparently growing fewer. Maybe people were going out of style.

Or whatever.

Needing to kill time, he thought about reclaiming the Urraco from the Park Lane underground car-park and revisiting some places he had liked in the old days—out in Kent, for example, where around Canterbury there were country pubs he recalled with vague nostalgia. Maybe that was worth doing; maybe it wasn't. He found himself half envying Irma for her pride at being constantly involved with the jet set, and even Bill, whose obsession with winning meant that he could get as excited over a videotape of the Cup Final as over the match itself in real time. But he himself had chosen to be a man of leisure. As the saying went, it had seemed like a good idea at the time . . .

Well, as the other saying went, having made his bed he had to lie in it.

But it would certainly help if he learned to lie more convincingly. Especially to himself.

THE city, though, seemed even less endurable than usual, with its hordes of child-beggars that he had to scatter with handfuls of change flung as far out into the roadway as he could manage. The technique always worked, because as soon as a fight broke out over who was to have the pound pieces, their attention magically switched, but it was still a damnable nuisance, and he was glad to see that the police were now patrolling in threes, one being a radio operator, so that trouble could be nipped in the bud. Moreover, there seemed to be a lot more of them than in the past.

But it was a shame there was so little traffic now. It might have run some of the greedy devils over.

After only a short while, therefore, he decided to collect the car and give himself a pleasanter impression of his homeland.

Part of Knightsbridge was closed; a neglected building had slumped into the road and enforced a detour, and the police had put up anti-looter barricades. Growing angrier by the minute, Godwin found himself constrained to walk to Marble Arch and approach by the northern end of Park Lane, where there had recently been a couple of bombings. The car-park, reportedly, was intact, but while of course even if it had not been he could have obtained another car without trouble, it would have been a nuisance, and nuisances were what he was least in the mood for.

The Global Hotel, at any rate, had escaped the bombers, and the commissionaire, Jackson, to whom he had been so generous in the recent past was on duty and chatting with a woman of about fifty, slender, wearing a bulky but lightweight black coat and black corduroy pants. Spotting Godwin just as he was about to cross the road and enter the car-park, he offered a salute and the woman beside him glanced around and time stopped.

It's impossible!
It's insane!
But if that little one whom I recall as Greer had lived to—

The thought snapped off like a dry branch. It was not palatable to think about the passage of time. He and his kind were outside it. When they needed repairs they were serviced more efficiently than a car could be. Time was not of their essence.

What we register is change. In the first flush of enthusiasm he had actually said that to somebody (who?) and known it was right and in consequence dismissed the matter for good and all.

No. More logical: in the course of a life any—even an ordinary—person sees so many other faces it must happen eventually that one recalls another.

Therefore he disregarded the commissionaire's attempt at signaling and, feigning not to have noticed, hastened toward the car-park, only to find that the entrance he meant to go down by was closed thanks to a bomb outrage, so he had to use another, further away.

More nuisance; more annoyance. He felt fuming.

But even worse: he felt scared. And that was not meant to be a possibility in his world. It was among the exclusions. Hastily he produced the car key from his pocket and showed it to the guards on duty at the barrier, noticing that they were armed with pistols; he registered change. Grumpy, they allowed him to proceed but warned that since he had left his car here for so long its tank might be empty, thanks to thieves.

Peasants!

It was, naturally, full. The familiar roar of the engine resounded comfortingly under the low concrete ceiling as he headed for the exit . . . from which, as he suddenly realized, he was compelled to turn north only. Hence he must again pass the front of the Global Hotel.

The charge plate he proffered when he drove out provoked satisfactorily raised eyebrows, but that was a minor consolation.

The same had happened often enough already to glut his capacity for being amused by it.

What dismayed him was that Jackson was still talking to the woman, and as soon as the Urraco appeared he pointed in its direction, and coincidentally there was an almost impossible event: a delay at the Oxford Street junction. It took two taxis and a bus and a collision between two vegetable-laden handcarts to create it . . . but it had long been a precept by which he abided that nothing in his world happened without there being a reason.

And there was no way he could avoid the woman's lingering stare, nor awareness of the change in her expression.

We register change . . .

By now he had half made up his mind that the simple erotic content of his latest memories accounted for his borderline obsession with fair-haired women; there had been other similar cases in the past, which wore away. But there was no mistake this time. She looked at him, and he recognized on her face an expression impossible to misinterpret.

I know you.

The jam had broken; a posse of police had arrived with braying sirens and overturned the interlocked carts, dumping their wares in the gutter, so that an instant flock of beggars and scavengers materialized and, for once tolerated, cleared the way. The taxis first, then his own car, then the bus, were waved past with urgent gestures implying that it would not matter in the slightest were a little animal matter mingled with the vegetables.

Godwin agreed, and accelerated eastward.

OXFORD Street having been for a long while closed to all traffic but buses and taxis, and in any case being beset by homeless hawkers, peddlers, and prostitutes, Godwin detoured via Wigmore Street and made his eventual way to Holborn and the slums of the City, where squatters swarmed like ants in the abandoned office blocks—some bombed, some burned for the insurance, some simply left to rot when the owning company collapsed. Hordes of ragged and filthy children rushed out to celebrate this rare event, the passage of a car, and when he halted more from force of habit than necessity at a blind junction, they converged on him screaming for money and displaying stump wrists and carefully cultivated sores.

He scared them off with a roar of his engine and thereafter crossed intersections without slowing, blasting his horn.

Thinking of Sittingbourne, he turned south to A2. In Greenwich an armed fascist patrol had set up a roadblock guarded by stern-faced boys with stolen army guns wearing Union Jack armbands on their black leather motorcycling jackets. Luckily a trio of policemen had paused to pass the time of day with them and someone had cracked a good joke which made them all chuckle. Barely glancing at him except to ensure he was white, they waved him by.

As darkness fell he arrived at his destination, a half-timbered rambling building which had been a coaching-inn and which the twentieth century had evolved into a roadhouse. It boasted a fabulous wine list, report said; Godwin dared not sample it, but he knew about its cuisine, and progressed through Whitstable native oysters via saddle of mutton with onion sauce and braised asparagus to steamed suet pudding and treacle, deferentially served by black-jacketed waiters to the accompaniment of quiet but unobtrusive music and the cheerful chatter of the other diners. The place was as crowded as he had ever seen it, but it was keeping up its standards. He overheard more than one person exclaiming over the superb quality of the red Bordeaux.

But even as Godwin was preparing to relax after his meal with a cigar and a cup of coffee, a familiar pressure started to build at the back of his mind. Annoyed, he attempted to dismiss it from consciousness; it was, of course, impossible. Somewhere, patience had come to an end.

And there was only one safe place to be when that happened. Home.

At least, he suspected that to be the case. He had never previously thought much about the question. But then, he had never before been other than eager for the reward it was his just entitlement to claim after a successfully completed assignment. The very idea of stalling would have puzzled him in the past—indeed, it was puzzling to him now, though he was all too hideously aware of the reason for his unprecedented reaction.

Damn Bill Harvey and his wartime recollections! *Damn* the blond woman in Park Lane!

He scribbled an illegible signature on the bill, having forgotten by what pseudonym they knew him here—not that it mattered, for none of his bills was ever presented for payment—and hastened back to the car, and back to London.

As though he were abruptly to be haunted by an earlier version of himself, so deeply buried in the past as to have been virtually forgotten, he realized as he approached his home that he was worrying about finding a parking space in his street. Never before had he left the Urraco at his own door. Without thinking much about the necessity to do otherwise, he had simply accepted it as risky, perhaps because of what had happened to other vehicles, the ruined Mark X Jaguar being only the latest of dozens. But the pressure in his head was increasing, and now it was peaking occasionally into pain and sending little bright shooting lights across his field of vision. He was going to have no time to do anything else.

Miraculously the very Jaguar he had been thinking about was gone when he drove cautiously around the corner, leaving a handy vacancy immediately in front of the house. He reversed into it thankfully and scrambled out without bothering to lock up.

Nobody would really touch his car, would they? Nobody ever had done. Not even during all that time in the Park Lane car-park when there were bomb scares and police investigations.

Anyway, what the hell? There could always be another!

Half blind with pain by now, he rushed upstairs and, not sparing time to turn the room on nor even to empty his bladder, he spent the last few moments of individual awareness trying desperately to reach a decision about his reward.

Then a dazzling inspiration struck him. Maybe he didn't have to choose. Maybe what had happened to undermine his last reward was a way of indicating that there were other possibilities he, with his limited imagination, had never thought of. Had Irma requested her Sirian plants? Had Hermann known in advance about Arikapanotulandaba's amazing powers? When had Hugo & Diana experienced free fall?

Thankful, convinced, he surrendered.

IT was dark. It was oppressively hot, but the air was dry. There was a stink of excrement. He ached in all his limbs, he was parched with thirst, his belly was acid with hunger, and there were sores around his wrists and ankles due to thick leather straps, first sewn and then riveted into place with copper rivets. Those on his legs hobbled him; those on his arms prevented him even reaching behind to cleanse himself after a motion. Also his scalp itched terribly.

He squatted on the floor of a room—no, a cell—too low for him to stand up, too narrow for him to lie down at full stretch. The posture in itself was not uncomfortable; all his life he had been accustomed to sitting on the ground. But he wished he could walk more than two strides.

More details impinged on his awareness. He wore a foul, greasy garment, too shapeless to be called a robe, which covered him from shoulders to knees. He was accustomed to sandals protecting his feet, but they were a forgotten luxury now. There were two small holes and one large in the walls and floor of his cell: one serving to piss and shit into, one admitting a little air—but it was so small, he could not even thrust his emaciated fist down it—and one closed with a heavy and expensive door, made of solid wood. The rest of the structure was of mud brick, not kiln-fired, not even baked, only sun-dried. But it was enough of an obstacle to contain such a weakling as a man.

From far away he heard the noise of a celebration: chanting, drumming, beating of cymbals, punctuated with loud laughter. His mouth turned bitterly down at the corners.

But that was ill-advised. That was stupid. That was dangerous. There was a reason why he was here—he firmly believed it—and it was his duty to endure patiently until understanding came. He forced his lips to shape a smile, and between gapped and aching teeth he hummed a sacred melody for the sake of its magical protective powers. A certain comfort came upon him as he repeated it over and over, lulling his consciousness into a state of vague, starvation-bred euphoria.

Abruptly he was aroused by the scraping of the wooden bars locking the cell door as they were drawn aside. He turned to face the entrance, rising to his knees.

The door creaked on its peglike hinges. In the opening was the jailer's bodyguard, club upraised. He believed the prisoner to be a sorcerer, and terribly dangerous. But he also believed in his club, and was proud of it, for it had been cut from a tree the like of which did not grow within seven days' journey. He had studded it with copper nails and around its narrower end he had bound leather strips for better purchase.

Behind him, though, came the jailer himself, wearing a relatively cleanly robe with an embroidered hem and a pair of costly copper bracelets.

"Come on, you!" he barked. "Got to make you fit to enter the king's presence!"

All of a sudden the prisoner realized the music had stopped while he was lost in his self-induced torpor. From the same direction there now came shouts and occasional wails of anguish.

Very interesting!

Stiffly, so he expected the creaking of his joints to be audible, he complied. He was hastened up a narrow passageway leading to a flight of much-worn stone stairs. At the top two women were waiting by the light of a rush-dip torch: one scrawny and middle-aged, one still youthful, both naked but for loincloths and bracelets. They had visibly been weeping; their eyes were red and swollen.

"Throw away that rag you're wearing!" barked the jailer. And, when the prisoner was slow to comply, ripped it from him.

"Rinse him down!" he ordered. "Anoint him with something that'll get rid of the stink! Hurry!"

The women had brought rags and pottery jars of clean water. With obvious distaste, for their services were not ordinarily misapplied to jailbirds, they slopped and sluiced away the worst of the dirt, then ladled perfumed oil on to his hair and beard and tore at the tangled locks with bone combs. A passable result was rapidly achieved, and the jailer, fretting, handed him a new robe, ankle-length, of blue cloth with red embroidery. Also his bodyguard produced a pair of sandals with leather thongs.

When he was presentable, he was hustled along another passageway and into a large courtyard, where he was surrendered into the charge of a guard captain, a burly man with a bronze sword, helmet and greaves, and bronze strips on his leather cuirass. He was accompanied by four taller men bearing long spears, like pikes, also helmeted, but with only epaulette plates on their cuirasses and short daggers in their belts instead of swords.

There was a formal exchange that included an oath or two. During it, the prisoner registered that the air stank of incense, roast meat, and terror in approximately equal proportions. He also saw that ahead of him, on the far side of the courtyard, there were several large windows beyond which torches shone and people's shadows moved. That was where the shouting was coming from, though it was not so loud by now.

The wailing and weeping, however, had proved contagious. It was being echoed from somewhere behind him, doubtless from other cells like his where hapless prisoners were confined in misery. It was amazing they had the strength to cry.

Then it was time for him to be taken into the royal presence and display his gifts as a soothsayer. With the guard captain ahead of him, two soldiers flanking and two following him, he limped across the irregular paving of the courtyard, resolving that the first thing he was going to demand when he entered the banqueting hall was a goblet of wine. And some decent bread, too, to mend the pangs in his belly. If this pagan despot wanted to use his services, he could damned well pay for them!

The prospect of bread and wine quite elevated his spirits, together with the sensation of clean cloth on his body and sound footgear under his abraded soles. He heard music beginning again and by reflex started to hum along, for he recognized it.

It was by William Walton.

It was *Belshazzar's Feast*.

Hurt, puzzled, dismayed, he halted in his tracks. Instead of colliding with him from behind, the soldiers following him froze like a stopped cinema film. So did those either side; so did the captain a pace ahead. It became impossible to move. The shifting shadows visible on the wall beyond the high windows, cast by flickering torches, became equally still. Everything turned into a fixed picture. Only his mind kept on functioning, though he was incapable of moving a single muscle. It was far worse than being confined in a cell, and it lasted for what felt like an eon. Then—

THEN it was worse still. He was taller, but he was also older, and instead of merely being chafed at wrists and ankles he had open, running sores; he had worn metal gyves until they were lately struck from him with such casualness he thought one of his wrist bones might be broken. He was completely naked, and did not need to glance down at himself to realize he was closer than ever to the verge of starvation.

The air was hot, but now with the full blast of a noontide sun, and it reeked not just with the stench of unwashed humanity but also with the fouler stink of rotting meat and new-spilled blood. He was in a barrel-shaped, vault-like room, shadowy but not cool, one end of which was blocked with the same two-palms-by-one fired brick that made up its ceiling-wall, the other being closed by a chained metal grille.

He was not alone. Slumped on the floor, or leaning with their backs against the wall in attitudes of unspeakable despair, were half a dozen men and women and two very young girls, not more than ten, all naked, all bruised and filthy. The girls were on either side of a woman who looked like their mother. It was obvious from their expressions and their tear-swollen eyes they wanted to hug her for what comfort the contact could provide; it was also plain that they dared not, for they were indecently unclad, and instead of reaching out with their hands they were using them to shield their private parts.

From outside, at intervals, could be heard screams, some of which were definitely not human, and the roar of a crowd brought to a peak of hysteria.

Someone, using a pebble or a smuggled stick, had managed to erode the outline of a fish into one of the softer bricks. One of the men was on his knees before this symbol and praying with all the force terror could lend him, except that not a sound emerged from his working lips.

The rest looked on as though they could not summon enough energy even to whisper.

More and different noise, much closer, heralded the arrival of four *lanistae*: all clad in rags, all armed with whips and sharp metal goads, one of them one-eyed and another one-armed. The two intact ones held great baying, slavering hounds on leashes.

The girl-children started to scream.

But with cuffs and kicks and jabs the *lanistae* roused the captives and herded them along a twisting tunnel, also closed by a grille, which at their approach was drawn aside. They were forced to emerge into the harsh sunlight of the arena called the Colosseum. They signed themselves and attempted futilely to strike up an audible hymn, but the roar of the crowd—loudest on the expensive side, where the spectators enjoyed awnings as a protection against the heat—drowned everything else, even the winding of *buccinae* as the editor of the games signaled for the next item.

A gang of slaves hurried out of the arena, wheeling with them carts which had served first to remove the carcasses from the last performance, then to bring clean sand while a musical interlude kept the throng entertained. But music was not what they had come here for.

A gust of laughter greeted the appearance of the captives, bare and helpless, and the emperor himself deigned to glance down from his box, where in fact a game of dice was occupying his attention. But on seeing that none of the victims was armed, and that a lion was being released from a cage on the far side, he lowered his emerald monocle and went back to something less predictable in its outcome.

The lion was nearly as ill-favored as the meal he was scheduled to enjoy. His tawny pelt was blotched with

some sort of eczema, and he favored his right front foot
as he looked about him, growling, in a posture halfway
between a crouch and getting ready to spring. The
crowd shouted louder than ever and people began to
toss empty wine jars and bits of broken masonry in the
hope of arousing the beast.

But instead of scenting food and rising to his full
height and pouncing, he looked vaguely puzzled for a
moment and then sat back and inspected his right fore-
paw. After licking it a couple of times, he looked again
at the huddled group of humans in front of him.

And purposefully, despite his limp, began to pad in
their direction, purring noisily.

He looked remarkably like a man in a lion's skin,
rather than a real lion.

Oh—no!

Shaw! Androcles who took the thorn out of the
lion's pad! The whole setup was so silly, he couldn't
help bursting into laughter. The laughter spread. First
his fellow Christians, whose identity he had no faintest
notion of, and then the watchful *lanistae* and the slaves
who surrounded the arena like banderilleros and pica-
dores at a bullfight . . . and then the crowd at large,
and ultimately the emperor himself were caught up in
the hysterical mirth.

Meantime the editor of the games fumed and
screamed and struck out insanely at his personal reti-
nue.

This also ground to a halt eventually.

Then—

HE was being helped to mount a bad-tempered horse. He felt like a lobster. He was encased in stiff, badly articulated armor bolted on his body over a thick, here and there quilted set of garments designed, apparently, to protect his most vital organs . . . but which were wholly revolting to the skin. They chafed; they itched abominably.

He could see very little of the world, for his head was boxed in by a clanging metal *sallade* and his view was obstructed by its visor.

Yet some thrilling chord in the depths of his being was touched by this predicament, as though he had proved in the ultimate analysis to be a bondage freak after all.

A person at the left edge of his field of vision took his left hand, which wore a clumsy plated gauntlet, and forced along his forearm a shield held in position with leather straps. Another person to his right, equally unrecognizable because the helmet acted like blinders, thrust a long, heavy, metal-tipped wooden pole into his grasp.

A lance? Yes, logically. But not nearly as well balanced as he had always imagined a lance to be. Trying to couch it against the back of his saddle—which itself was by no means a masterpiece—so that the brunt of an impact would be transferred to the greater mass of the horse, he found there was far too much of it still ahead of the pivotal point at which he was constrained to grasp it. It was going to wave about like a ship's mast in a gale.

But it was much too late to worry about that kind of

thing. His attendants, screaming with terror, were vanishing into the surrounding woodland . . .

Woodland?

As best he could he surveyed the scene. This was a glade in hilly but well-forested country, and there were chiefly birch, ash, and beech trees to be seen. It had recently been raining: the nearby rocks—which looked like granite—were glistening, and the grass underfoot was damp and marshy.

And a noise was coming from somewhere out of sight which was causing his steed to whinny and back, provoking a reflex jerk on the reins and a jab of both heels into the sides of his poor mount. He was clearly not the finest one could wish for; though he was stocky and broad-hoofed, he was fitter to haul a cart or drag a plow than carry a knight-at-arms into battle. He was half bald, and—

Battle?

Still thinking about the horse's mange-gnawed mane, the rider listened again to the noise, partway between a roar and a howl, which had so upset the beast. This time it provoked a curvet, a caracole and a turnabout, all done without schooling, which bid fair to unseat him. He found himself facing in the opposite direction before he could regain control.

And there, dead ahead of him, was a nearly naked girl tied to the face of a smooth gray rock. She was overweight for her age—about fifteen—and her hair was hanging in sweaty strands either side of her fat, ill-tempered face, and her fat hands had clawed at the rock until the nails were rimmed with red, and she had shat herself with terror and the thin yellow garment which was all she wore revealed the news to the world only too plainly.

As it began to crisp around the edges in the blasting-hot breath of a creature waddling toward her on scaly legs with claw-tipped toes like an overgrown cockerel's, its body patched with lurid yellow and green like an attack of luminescent fungi, its head on a serpentine neck weaving back and forth with its maw not just blood-red as it gaped, but *glowing* red, and instead of arms or forelegs or forelimbs, a pair of totally unbelievable scarlet wings, as formal as a lady's fan.

Half Uccello, half—someone else's. Confused. But with the ill-assorted mix still identifiable. It did not require him to turn his shield to realize that it would be white with a red cross.

What were these bastards and sons-of-bitches trying to *do* to him? This wasn't funny. This was a mockery!

And a great welling flood of black, unadulterated fury erupted from the depths of his being. The scene tried to freeze. It didn't have time (curious that he should think in terms of the scene as autonomous—but since obviously it could never have occurred in reality, perhaps it was so).

Instead, it melted: each patch of color, like wax, blending into another; like the contrasts of children's modeling clay rolled into a ball, it ended in a flat brownish-gray mess in the midst of which he was embedded, unable either to move or to reason. He felt that someone's back had been turned on him: that a Power had offered him the best that was to be had, and he—through stupidity or ill-temper or perverseness—had rejected it.

He felt, and knew, that he was damned.

It was very much worse than the pangs of punishment. It divorced him from his body, from his essence, from any semblance of anything he might believe in as reality.

It went on and on, as though he had been flung aside and then forgotten.

HE came to himself feeling that he had rather been possessed than rewarded. He ached dreadfully; he was very cold; his belly was sour and his head throbbed and he had clenched his hands into suffering fists for so long, his nails felt as though they had begun to grow into his palms. He fought with all his feeble force to avoid thinking of it, but he was inexorably reminded of the days—so far in the past, it was like trying to remember with someone else's brain, yet simultaneously it was as real as yesterday—when this was his ordinary state on waking.

He wanted to weep, but his eyes were obstinately dry. Instead he undertook the terrible effort first of unfolding his fingers, then of turning into a sitting position on the edge of the bed to look about him.

Beyond the window he saw bright sunlight and blue sky with a few scudding clouds. But the room, inactive, looked gray and dingy and neglected. One of the taps over the cracked sink was dripping for want of a new washer, and had left an iron-brown stain on the china. The mirror above was fly-specked with age. A spider had woven a complex web from the towel rail to the corner of the shower cabinet.

It would have taken only a slight effort to turn the room on again, but he was either too weak or too full of self-loathing to make the necessary decision. He hoped it was only the former. He had been lying still for a long, long while. His face and hands felt positively dusty, paralleling the foulness in his memory.

Eventually he was able to do something about his predicament. Regardless of complaints from all his muscles, he forced himself to his feet, stripped off his clothes, and stepped into the shower. The water was cold and the soap had turned to a jellied mess in its dish, but he found paradoxical relief in inflicting punishment on himself. He rubbed down with a greasy and overused towel and scrubbed his teeth until his gums bled, but felt he had made some sort of expiation when he turned at last to the wardrobe, planning to dress, get out of here, and find something to eat. He never kept provisions at home, and if he had had any, they would be spoiled by this time, and besides—perhaps for the same indefinable reason he didn't care to switch on the room—he wanted something plain and dull and crude, like sandwiches of greasy bacon between doorsteps of bread washed down with hot, sweet tea.

The wardrobe, naturally, was empty. He had nothing to put on except what he had taken off: stylish, lightweight, uncomfortable, designed for a single wearing. In particular the shoes hurt his feet.

But he had to dress.

Reluctantly he did so, and slipped out of his room like a cautious burglar. TV noise came from below, but there was nobody in sight. He made it to the street, though afraid the nausea churning in his belly might provoke a fit of vomiting . . . if there was anything to vomit.

Just as he was drawing the front door shut behind him, he noticed the Urraco and remembered with a shock that he had been compelled to park it here instead of at his usual garage. But he had no time to worry about it at present. It looked all right—hadn't been splashed with paint or acid, or broken into, or had its tires slashed—and that would have to do for the time being. He turned the other way.

At precisely that moment another car which he had not spotted, or at any rate not paid attention to, pulled to a halt a couple of yards ahead of him and a man with a brown mustache, wearing an old-fashioned khaki raincoat, emerged from it and confronted him. Simultaneously another man, younger, in a blue sweater and jeans, got out by the rear door and warily approached, while the driver muttered something into a hand-held microphone.

"Chief Inspector Roadstone," the man in the raincoat said, flashing a warrant card. "I have reason to believe your name is Godfrey Harper and that car there, the Lamborghini, belongs to you. I want to ask you a few questions."

For a moment Godwin was at a total loss. His head swam. Of all the times for something like this to happen . . . ! And it had been so long since the last occasion, too, that he had half forgotten the knack of dealing with such problems.

Except he hadn't. Seconds later the flex came back to him, the technique which he had learned from Ambrose Farr longer ago than he could recall. Experience had taught him to avoid it, for it was invariably tiring, but now it seemed he had no alternative. He was out on the open street, and—the message about the intrusion of police having spread like magic—being stared at by half a hundred people, some on the pavement, some leaning out of windows. Besides, insofar as such a person existed at all, he was indeed Godfrey Harper; it was convenient to have an alias when it came to such things as registering a car on which no taxes had ever been paid.

The question stood, though: was he strong enough in his present state to work the flex?

Sweating, trembling, he concluded he must find out the hard way.

Summoning all his remaining resources, fighting the nausea which threatened to overwhelm him at any moment, focusing his attention on all three of the policemen but unable to cope with the bystanders and obliged to leave them to chance, he said in a peculiarly soft, wheedling tone, "There is no such person as Godfrey Harper. I am not Godfrey Harper. Nobody is Godfrey Harper. That car is mine. It belongs to me. It is legitimately mine. You have come here on a wild-goose chase. There was no point in coming here. When you get back to your police station you will enter these facts in your official report. You will go back to the police station right away and report that it was a false alarm that brought you here and it was all a waste of time. You will make an entry in PNC to ensure that in future nobody will waste time checking Godfrey Harper because Godfrey Harper does not exist."

His voice was on the edge of breaking, so intense was his concentration, but he recognized the working of the flex: the three men were relaxing, nodding to one another, beginning to smile.

Eventually Roadstone said with a shrug, "Sorry to have wasted your time, sir. But I'm sure you realize we get these malicious calls occasionally, and we have to investigate. We'll head straight back to the Yard and make sure no one else bothers you unnecessarily."

"That's quite all right—I understand."

"Good morning!"

"Good morning to *you*."

He forced an affable smile and stood watching while they returned to the car and drove away. Then, and only then, he let go a colossal gasp of relief. His nausea had vanished with the successful deployment of the flex, but now he was so hungry he felt afraid of fainting; also he craved great mugfuls of that sweet and scalding tea he had previously only thought wistfully about. Now it had become like an obsession, and the nearest place he could be sure of finding it was a squalid little caff, stinking of burned fat, within two or three minutes' fast walk of here. He was poised to take the first step . . .

When he realized that watching him from shadow beside what had been the handsome front porch of a house on the far side of the street and was now boarded in to make more or less weatherproof accommodation for stray children the landlord had taken pity on, stood the blond woman he had seen talking to the commissionaire outside the Global Hotel.

The one he thought he recognized against all odds.
The one he was certain had recognized him.

For a frozen second they stared at one another. But
this encounter made no more sense than the other. She
remained as still as though he had exercised the flex on
her. But he had not, and very definitely he now could
not; he had squandered all his energy on the three policemen.

Godwin realized with sick horror that he must do
something he had not done for ages.

Trust to luck.

Though the sky was bright and the sun was shining,
the air today was chill. With violent abruptness he
turned up his jacket collar and strode off toward the
sanctuary of the caff, not looking back to see what the
woman did.

As he went he found he was shivering more fiercely
than the edge on the wind could explain.

IN the entrance of the caff a one-legged man in a greasy black overcoat was standing guard. He had two crutches: with one he kept his balance; with the other—and a volley of curses—he kept at bay the usual horde of lousy and shivering urchins. Now and then he also drove away an adult, if he or she looked particularly dirty, shabby, or sick. He seemed for a moment minded to challenge Godwin, but by the standards of this area he was finely dressed, and despite his unshaven face with dark rings under the eyes he looked in exceptionally good health. Such a one was certain to have enough money to pay for what he ordered, though naturally it was a mystery what he was doing here.

Relieved, Godwin stepped over the threshold into relative warmth, only to realize with a wrenching shock as he took his place in line at the counter that in fact he did not have any money, or at any rate no cash. He had grown accustomed to tossing change at beggars to disperse them, and his pockets were empty except for his wallet.

But there were credit-card stickers on the electronic cash register which was the only new and smart thing about the place, and his heart ceased to pound. He ordered the sausage-and-bacon sandwich which he had been craving, and the mug of tea, and proffered his cards like a poker hand, noticing with vague interest that the indicated limit on each had risen to a thousand pounds. He scrawled a signature that more or less matched the one on the card which the weary-faced proprietress selected, and turned away with his laden tray in search of somewhere to sit down.

The clientèle of the caff was divided into four recognizably separate groups. Nearest the door, where they were most easily got rid of if occasion arose, there were ill-clad elderly men and women with greasy lank gray hair, doing their utmost to make one mug of tea last all day, not speaking among themselves but occasionally passing a precious cigarette. Behind them, sharing a mound of steak-and-kidney pies, sat six or seven flash young street people doubtless blowing the proceeds of a successful dip or mugging, since they could not possibly have afforded so much meat otherwise. Beyond them again were a cluster of respectable clerkly men and women, mostly in early middle age, with the dull look of disillusionment on their faces which characterized out-of-work computer programmers and the like, pretending that it was no more than sensible economy which persuaded them to lunch here off a wedge of cheese, a bread roll, and a glass of water. Two or three had, on cheekbones or wrists, the long-lasting subcutaneous hemorrhages indicative of scurvy.

The atmosphere of the place, quite apart from the stench of overused frying oil which pervaded it, came close to making Godwin turn back to the counter and ask for his food and drink to be transferred into takeaway packs. But there was a kind of buffer zone at the rear of the caff, beyond the clerkly ones, where a whole rank of vacant seats divided the mere customers from the permanent occupants: all men, all prosperous-looking, one of them presumably the husband of the tired and snappish woman at the counter, smoking cigars and passing an illegal bottle of whisky—this place had no liquor license. They exuded the calm security of people in control. One of them, recognizing the expensive cut of Godwin's clothes, deigned to give a curt nod toward the vacant row, according him permission to sit there, as though because from him at least it was improbable he and his companions would contract fleas.

Grateful, though at a loss, Godwin complied and wolfed down his meal. The men nearby said nothing he could hear, yet it was plain there was communication going on. They appeared to be waiting for something to happen, but in no hurry for it.

After a while, as the food made a hot mass in his belly, his sluggish mind revived. Little by little he realized with dismay that he had inadvertently done something he had long guarded against. To the best of his belief, now that the flex had taken care of the three policemen, the blond woman across the street was the only person in the world, apart from such as Gorse— about whom, naturally, he had no need to worry—who had reason to connect him with the place where he lived. The neighbors and transients who infested his home street did not count, for that or anything.

But . . .

It was absolutely and completely impossible, he was sure, that he could have recognized her. Yet the congruence between her mature, adult face and the face he so clearly recalled from the setting of the Blitz (the crump of explosions, the rumble of collapsing buildings, the hiss and crackle of flames, the dust so thick in the nostrils of memory it threatened to make him sneeze) was incredibly perfect! Had he seen her somewhere, long ago, and stored up an image which the reward drew from his subconscious to make the experience seem that much more real?

That explanation was plausible, but it did not *feel* true.

Was his remembered experience real in some halfway sense? It could not be objectively so—Bill Harvey had demolished all hope of him being able to pretend that it was, but in any case he had always been content to enjoy the benefit of his rewards without inquiring too deeply into the way they were created—yet perhaps it had taken place at some kind of skew-wiff angle between the main line of reality and the diffuse worlds of simple fantasy.

He trembled. He was unused to thinking in these terms. He had done so when he first began to live the life he had chosen, but gradually the habit of enjoying what he had offered himself took over. He had endured unquestioningly for . . .

No, it was not to be thought about, even now. How the hell could Bill bear to count his birthdays? He gulped the rest of his tea and reverted to a simpler but more pressing matter. There was no doubt at all why it was wrong to let somebody know both who he was and where he was living. All this was explicable on the plain human level. There were things like taxes, justifying your expenditure, keeping medical records, entering data in computers, applying for passports, driving cars, and more and ever more interlocking networks of information between the interstices of which he must continue to keep slithering. All this was automatic—or had been. Suddenly, dismayingly, he was faced with the need to take even more action than just using the flex. Until he had done so, he knew he would continue to feel . . . would the right term be uncomfortable?

Maybe that was why his attempt to enjoy a reward chosen at random had failed. Maybe it was because he had been less-than-consciously aware of the risk he was running from the moment he saw the blond woman talking to the commissionaire and nonetheless drove the Urraco out of the car-park in full sight of where they were standing. Now there were so few cars in London, the mere possession of one was a marker. Having chosen such a rare model compounded the difficulty.

Simultaneously he felt relief and renewed dismay: the former, because he had reasoned out his predicament and decided to take action, even though as yet he did not know what kind; the latter, because as he rose and headed for the exit—where the one-legged man was leaning on both crutches and extending a hand for the tip which was his due for saving the customers from being importuned by beggars—something reported from his stomach the need to visit Luke. Scarcely surprising. Hygiene here was rudimentary. Flies swarmed on sugar bowls; food was handed to purchasers with unwashed hands; cups and dishes were rinsed in cold and often greasy water because of the cost of fuel; the

display of sandwiches and salads remained until someone was fool enough to buy because it was prohibitively
costly to throw away anything remotely edible.

Why the hell had he come here, anyway? Already
memory of the state he had been in when he rose had
receded to the same blur as those other memories,
masked and blanketed and overlaid, which he was so
determined to hide from himself, the reasons why he
would never take the least sip of alcohol except in the
security of his home.

He was suffused with a pang of gratitude for the
good care that was being taken of him. But he had no
money to tip the door guard.

Oh, never mind! He had just realized he knew where
to go from here. Not directly to Luke, because under-
used though they were, his body's immune reactions
and other defenses were in fine fettle, thanks to Irma's
regular attention, so for a while he could afford to dis-
regard that particular impulse.

No. He must visit Hamish.

The decision clicked in his mind and he strode past
the guard as though the man did not exist, nor anybody
else who could not contribute to making their encounter
more immediate.

DENSE and stinking fog that made the eyes water—
a real London pea-souper—closed in around Godwin
as he approached the home-cum-office of Hamish
Kemp. Here and there gas lights glimmered though it
was midafternoon, creating fragile bubbles of lumi-
nance lost almost as soon as sighted through the murk.
The air resounded with the clatter of hooves, the rattle
of iron-tired cab wheels over cobblestones, the continu-
ing tintinnabulation of bicycle bells madly rung by er-
rand boys terrified of punishment were they late with
a single delivery. Now and then there was an acci-
dent, invisibly far away; old ladies screamed and cats
yowled and shouts were raised to find the nearest
chemist's shop for the injured. Small wonder. Godwin
could literally not see his own hand at arm's length.

Fortunately his feet remembered better than his
head, and at no worse cost than a sense of clammy chill
due to fog droplets penetrating his unsuitable clothes
and being half blinded with tears owing to the sulfurous
reek of a million coal fires, he attained Hamish Kemp's
door. It opened to his touch . . . naturally.

The air inside was crystal clear. He stepped onto
deep-piled Persian rugs; on either side enormous overstuffed chairs with leather or tapestry upholstery stood
ready to welcome visitors, grouped around low tables
set with tantaluses and wire-encaged refillable soda sy-
phons. Paintings by Landseer and—daringly—Alma-
Tadema hung on walls papered with designs by William
Morris. Here stood a whatnot with the indefinable stamp
of Mackintosh of Edinburgh, on which reposed a humi-
dor containing fine Havana cigars; there, a radiant

electric heater with five elements—each containing a twisted red-glowing wire within an evacuated glass envelope like an oversize and misshapen banana—shed welcome warmth across a tiled hearth innocent of ashes. A glass-fronted cabinet, with locked doors, stood against one wall, containing an Afghan *jezail,* a Snyder, a pair of dueling pistols with ivory-inlaid handles, a snaphaunce flintlock, and a blunderbuss. More practical weapons were stored, of course, out of sight.

There appeared to be no one in the gas-lit room. Godwin, whose meal was now more and more insistently announcing that it was about to disagree with him and who consequently was more and more driven to leave at once and go consult Luke, lost patience and shouted at the top of his voice.

"Hamish!"

Panels at the far end of the room folded back to reveal a white-walled, stark, chrome-and-stainless-steel-and-glass laboratory where Hamish, clad in a green surgical gown and mask, was rising from a revolving chair before a complex instrument board, beset with TV screens, switches, buttons, scales, analogue dials, warning lights, and digital counters. He was a portly man with a somewhat florid face, sporting muttonchop whiskers. When he doffed his gown it was to reveal a striped-on-white flannel shirt minus its collar and studs, the trousers of a brown tweed suit, and brown boots.

Sighing, he said, "Yes, God. I deduced you or somebody was about to bother me. It had better be urgent or else—"

A shrill noise interrupted him, which came from the far end of the lab. Both men reflexively glanced that way. A section of wall had slid aside, revealing clear black sky beyond . . . or its image. Across the velvet-dark oblong a bright disc wavered, for all the world like a paper plate tossed Frisbee-fashion. Suddenly it plunged toward them. The shrill noise ceased. A deep-toned bell chimed once. The wall closed again. There was a succession of loud clicks, which Hamish, head on one side, counted in anxious fashion.

At length he breathed a sigh of relief.

"Lucky I just finished automating that part of the machinery!" he said in a loud and accusing tone. "Not for you nor anyone would I forgo the pleasure I derive from my sole hobby nowadays, pointless though it may seem to you and your kind! Have a *chota peg*?" he added, as by afterthought, and waved Godwin to one of the overstuffed chairs.

Godwin shook his head, while—seeming to have forgotten the offer—Hamish served himself a generous four fingers of whisky and baptized the glass with a sprinkle of soda-water.

Sitting down in turn, while the laboratory faded from view, Hamish said, "Now have you the least idea where that—that disc you saw had been to?"

Godwin shook his head, wondering how long this preamble would last. This wasn't the Hamish he remembered—

Correction. It could be no one else.

We register change.

Conceivably he had made one of the stupidest mistakes of his entire life by coming here.

But who else could he possibly have turned to?

And Hamish was saying with a kind of triumph, "No more do I! But I shall know, tomorrow at the latest! I send out hundreds of them all the time, and some of them are smashed by storms and some go on such a huge and random trajectory they may not find their way home for years—for decades! Some may come back in the far and distant future, because when I say they were driven down by storms that is, remember, only an assumption! My current record is one which went on flying for over eleven years, signaling in emergency mode for most of the time—that makes them luminous, you understand! *That* one informed me precisely where it had visited! You appreciate they carry no instrumentation? They are simply what they are— discs cast out into the wild blue yonder, to fly and home as chance decrees. And each that returns bears with it clues to where it wandered. By tonight I shall know whether that latest one to arrive has crossed the Arctic ice or the grainfields of Canada or the industrial Ruhr. Ah, you've no idea how fascinating, how endlessly fascinating it is to deduce from such tiny hints, such scraps of data, the entire course of an object which has traveled thousands upon thousands of miles."

He sounded as though he were trying to convince himself as much as his listener. But when he had gulped down the last of his drink, he set the glass aside and at once became briskly businesslike.

"Well! It doesn't take a detective to work out that you came here because something has gone wrong. Conceivably something to do with your last assignment? In which case, obviously, I can't intervene."

"No, it isn't that. I want you to trace somebody for me. A woman."

Hamish raised one bushy eyebrow. "A woman, eh? I had no idea you were so susceptible. I understood you were always well provided for."

"You don't generally jump to conclusions," Godwin said cuttingly. "Shall I explain?"

Hamish sighed and leaned back, closing his eyes.

When he had heard his visitor out, he gradually began to smile. By the time he finally reopened his eyes he was positively beaming.

"This is a problem worthy of my mettle, indeed! You know of only two people that this woman knows: the commissionaire, who may have met her on a single occasion and never have heard mention of her name, and this policeman Roadstone—perhaps. In the ordinary run of events we could simply ask him. But this is not ordinary. You have used the flex on him and his colleagues, and in consequence they are no longer even able to think about the matter. But you're quite right. You do need to trace her and, as it were, eliminate any threat."

"I don't want to eliminate her. Why should I?"

"I said eliminate any threat," Hamish corrected.

"Use the flex on her too, perhaps. With the techniques that the forces of the ungodly have at their disposal nowadays, it would be fatal if even a breath of suspicion were to get about." He had no need to describe what kind of suspicion. Witch burnings might be out of date; witch hunts most definitely were not.

"Still," he continued, hoisting himself ponderously to his feet, "we have resources of our own. Come into the laboratory and we'll work out a portrait of her."

Godwin complied. Standing in front of a computer-controlled image-creation system, Hamish called up detail on a screen while Godwin corrected his approximations. He muttered as he worked.

"Fair—slim—about how tall? Five six, seven? Hair not so far down the forehead, right . . . Nose not so long? How about that?"

Within a matter of minutes there was a full-color picture on the screen which matched Godwin's recollection almost flawlessly. Relieved, and increasingly in a hurry to visit Luke, he nonetheless hesitated before turning away.

"There's one thing still not right," he admitted reluctantly.

Hamish chuckled. "I know," he said, and made some minute adjustments to the face. "What you were asking for was the face of a little girl, a mere child. That makes her look her age, doesn't it?"

Godwin nodded, suppressing a shiver.

"Fine!" Hamish tapped an instruction into the keyboard below the screen, and the image vanished. "We have something to work from, at any rate. There's a chance her picture may be on file—I have over a million news photographs, to start with, and the machines are already sifting through them. But it's bound to be a slow job, I'm afraid. Now if you take my advice"— ushering Godwin toward the door—"you won't go home for the next few days. Find somewhere else to put up. The fact that she actually saw you coming out of the house is what disturbs me most. Incidentally, how about the car?"

"Still where I left it. Did you expect me to drive here?"

"No, but . . . Well, I'm sure you can detect whether or not you're being followed, particularly in light traffic. Put it in a popular garage—the Soho Lex would do—and make a detour through some large and busy department store with several exits. And do it as soon as possible."

"I need to visit Luke first," Godwin said after a brief pause. Hamish threw up his hands.

"Dear, oh dear! And I understood Irma took such good care of you! At least she always boasts that she does when I call on her. Well, as and when you can. And I'll contact you as soon as I have anything definite to report."

"Have you any idea how long it might take?"

"None whatever, my dear fellow—none whatever! After all, on the information you've given me she may perfectly well be an Australian visitor in London for a couple of days."

"Why should an Australian come with the police to find me?"

"Perhaps she works for Melbourne CID and you're the going-double of a wanted drug smuggler! How should I know? Really, God, you do expect miracles, don't you? I grant, I'm often in a position to work one, but on something this flimsy—no, I must have time. But I promise you, I shall get on with it straight away, and it will enjoy my undivided attention. That is, unless I unexpectedly find myself otherwise engaged, as it were."

"Is that likely?"

"Well, it has been quite some while, so there's rather a high probability. However, there's no need for you to worry about that."

His tone meant "pry into that." Godwin, slightly embarrassed, shook hands and left. Hamish called after him, "Give my regards to Luke, won't you?"

"Yes, of course. And thank you!"

DR. Luke Powers received his client in a room completely bare except for a couch draped in white, a green carpet on the floor, and on one wall a beautifully hand-lettered scroll with illuminated margins bearing the full text of the Hippocratic oath in the original Greek. He was a lean, ascetic man whose age might have been anything from thirty to fifty but almost certainly wasn't, with piercing gray eyes deep-set above a neatly trimmed brown beard.

"Welcome," he said, and his voice was resonant and thrilling. He made no offer to shake hands, but stood stock-still with his total attention fixed on Godwin while the latter undressed. There were hooks, hangers, and a rail on the back of the door.

"You ate something inadvisable," the healer said at length. "Not only was the food of poor quality and rather stale, it was heavily contaminated with chemical adulterants. Lie down. It's as well you came to me now rather than later—I feel the urge to retire from the world and meditate. But I think there may be time to put you right. Close your eyes."

He laid both hands on Godwin's abdomen and began to murmur under his breath. The queasiness, which had become acute by now, dissipated; a painful bubble of wind passed a resistant sphincter; what little goodness and nourishment there was in Godwin's meal entered his system while the remainder was securely locked up until it was time for it to be expelled.

"There," Luke said after five or six minutes. "You may dress again now. But be careful, God. You ought to know by this time that, living the way we do, we risk allowing our natural defense mechanisms to atrophy." The last word concluded in a yawn, for which, with a chuckle, he apologized as soon as he could.

"Even though that was relatively quickly dealt with," he added, "I find the process extremely tiring. You'll excuse me if I simply take your place on the couch and ask you to see yourself out?"

"Of course," Godwin muttered, zipping up his trousers and silently wondering why everybody except himself seemed unable or unwilling to accept the truth but must always disguise it by some such term as meditation or communion with the infinite or seeking astral guidance. They must know what was going on! After all, they invariably recognized the term when he referred to being called . . .

But he had more urgent matters to consider, such as moving the car. He took his leave of Luke and headed homeward.

HE was half hoping the fair woman would be watching the house again. It would simplify matters if he let her find him; after Luke's treatment he was sufficiently recovered to use the flex on her, and if he got the chance that would be an end of the matter.

However, there was no one in the street exhibiting more than casual curiosity when he climbed into the Urraco. He started up and drove a quarter of a mile, keeping an eye on his mirror, but no one was following.

Now: where to go? After the infuriating disappointment of his last reward, he felt the need for some sort of relaxation, but he didn't want to go abroad again on the same passport, even though on his last trip no one had asked to see it.

Just as he was dutifully parking the car in the Lex garage in Soho, as Hamish had instructed, inspiration dawned. He snapped his fingers. Of course—the Global Hotel. The chance of the Arab princes still being there was vanishingly small; in any case, if they or the discothèque staff took exception to his presence, he was fit enough to use the flex again. And a suitable bribe would surely persuade Jackson the commissionaire to relate whatever he knew about the fair woman, so the data could be relayed to Hamish.

And conceivably the woman herself might turn up.

BUT she didn't, and nobody at the hotel paid him special attention except for people working in the discothèque—which turned out to be an independent, subcontracted operation—who scowled at him or beamed according to which of his visits they remembered him from. And Jackson had simply failed to arrive for work today, so they had hired someone else. There was always a long waiting list for his kind of job. Come to that, there was a waiting list for any job. Perhaps he had been mugged or stabbed on the way home; perhaps he had been run over; perhaps he had contracted one of the countless epidemics permanently infesting any large city; at all events, he had not been seen or heard from. Computer investigation on the scale accessible to Godwin failed to trace him. He passed the information to Hamish and hoped for the best.

Which was what he personally was not enjoying. The Global Hotel was luxurious on its own level, but compared to his home it was boring. To wake every morning in the same room with the same outlook was unbearably monotonous. Worse yet, he was waking from unrestful sleep; his dreams were haunted by the dust-and-ashes taste of his last "reward." He was puzzled and hurt by what had happened, not during the experiences, but afterwards, during that immeasurable period when he had felt forgotten, abandoned, neglected, thrown aside. He suspected why and how that had come about, but he was mortally afraid of spelling it out to himself, and did whatever he could think of to avoid confronting his own conclusions.

He regarded it as something of an achievement when

finally he admitted to himself that it had not been indigestion which had taken him to Luke, but a terrible feeling like a vast bruise.

Which Luke had not diagnosed or referred to. Or treated.

Why?

Frustrated, dispirited, anxious to an extent he had imagined would never be his lot again, he passed the time as best he could. Eventually idleness grew unbearable, and he decided to do something he had never done before: call on Bill Harvey and inquire after Gorse. Ordinarily he felt no more than a faint pang of curiosity about those he had recruited; now and then he realized he must have opposite numbers—a woman who recruited boys, a man and a woman who recruited gays—but the matter had always seemed so inconsequential until now that he had automatically dismissed it.

Or else, perhaps, the illusive reality of the reward experience which followed an assignment masked any burgeoning interest.

But he was in no state to reason out problems of that magnitude. He was growing more and more obsessed with the unprecedented anomaly which the fair woman represented. He had searched his memory over and over, attempting to locate some chance encounter, some situation, which could have given him the image around which might have developed his conviction that he recognized her, and that she was the adult counterpart of the little girl in his George Medal experience.

But how could she be? He had checked up on what Bill had told him, and it was true: he had been given a decoration which did not yet exist. Had he been at home he would have ripped the medal from his cabinet of mementos and flung it in the dustbin along with its "authenticating" press cutting . . . except that their destruction would have had to be more thorough, medals being remarkable even to dustmen. The function of such souvenirs was to persuade him, even for a little while, that his remembered experiences were real so far as he was concerned. To have one which at every glance must inform him it was a snare and a deception—it was intolerable!

Therefore he must find ways of not thinking about it. Possibly contact with someone as down-to-earth as Bill Harvey would be helpful in distracting him. Bill, after all, except for his enjoyment of telerecorded football matches and horse races, lived wholly in the present, as Godwin usually did—as he had imagined had become automatic with him. Reviewing the past had grown painful, or at least uncomfortable.

And perhaps if Gorse were not doing anything else they might make love. He recalled her capacity for orgasm. It had been impressive.

Not that any twice-tasted fruit could possess the same appeal.

AT the very moment he reached the front steps of Bill's home, the door opened and Gorse came out. She was wearing the height of fashion: a wide-shouldered barathea blouse, a skirt slashed into irregular ribbons, boots stained camouflage green and brown. On what little could be seen of her face around immense dark glasses there was an expression of grim determination. For an instant Godwin feared she might have been called, in which case it would be pointless to address her, but halfway down the steps she seemed to start noticing the outside world, and as she came level with him she checked, removed the glasses, and said, "Oh, it *is* you."

Her face was not so much pale as gray; it was drawn, it was haggard. Even before she spoke again Godwin could guess what she was about to say.

"Can't stop—sorry. I have to go see somebody called Irma. Bill gave me the address."

"Just a second!"

"I said I can't stop!" Then, relenting: "Oh, very well. What is it?"

"How do you feel about—well, you know?"

"Oh!" Her red-rimmed eyes lit up. "Oh, it's fantastic! It's the kind of thing I've been looking for all my life without realizing! People who join secret societies like the Rosicrucians or the Freemasons or the Illuminati must be looking for exactly what you've given me! And not getting half such a bargain! You're a darling, and thank you very much!" She pursed her lips and planted a sketch for a kiss on his cheek. "But I have to rush! And you of all people must understand why!"

So that was going to be her justification to herself. Well, it was at least a variation on a theme . . .

He watched her until she vanished around the corner in a flurry of ragged-robin skirts, and only then realized that Bill—tankard in hand as ever—was standing on the front doorstep, gazing thoughtfully his way.

Godwin walked up to join him.

"Glad she got the chance to go see Irma," Bill said reflectively, ushering him inside. There were more luck charms than ever on display in the hallway, including a collection of new white bones hanging from red and yellow cords. "The way she's been working 'erself . . . ! Same as with an 'orse, y'know. Overtraining, they call it. Result: you get the peak performance day before the race, an' your favorite comes in nowhere! Come in the parlor. Good to see yer. Fancy a jar?"

"You know I don't," Godwin said as the parlor engulfed him: a dark place full of overstuffed Victorian furniture, bric-à-brac displays, velvet drapes tied back with thick gold cords, almost the only modern note being struck by the TV set and its attached recorder. One entire wall was taken up by a bar whose display would not have disgraced a pub.

"Well, I bloody know you didn't come round to watch my tape of yesterday's Prudential match!" Bill said tartly, dropping into an armchair and waving his guest to do the same. "What is it? Got under your skin, did she—the little one?"

"I don't think so," Godwin said after a hesitation. "No, to be honest I came to ask you a question."

"So let's be 'earin' from yer!"

"Are you satisfied with what you've got?"

The words were out before he could check them. It had been in his mind to ask a different question, but it seemed of secondary importance compared to what he had just said.

Bill's face darkened. "Wotcher mean?"

"Well . . ." A helpless gesture. "Well, if they won't let you in the betting shop any more, for example. Doesn't it sort of spoil something in life for you?"

Contemptuously: "If they won't listen to me, let 'em rot! Lord, between us we could've cleaned up . . . But they won't, so the 'ell with 'em. Far's I'm concerned, I'm livin' the life of Riley, an' if me mates don't want a share, they don't 'ave to 'ave one. What's turned *you* so sour all of a sudden?"

"I . . ." Godwin licked his lips. "Bill, what would you do if you thought somebody had sussed you out?"

"Like for instance?"

"Well, the police."

"Flex 'em, wot else? I never 'ad no trouble with the rozzers! Nor the buggers in the tax-office neither, though they was persistent for a while. 'Ere! Y'know something?"

He leaned forward earnestly, eying Godwin with disapproval.

"I don't like wot you're implyin'! You run acrost somebody you can't flex out?"

"I was sort of tired when it happened, and I didn't catch on until later," Godwin said in a self-exonerating tone.

"Hah! I still don't like it! With that on yer back, yer didn't oughta come 'ere, did yer?"

"I've done what I can. I put Hamish Kemp on it right away—"

" 'Im?" Bill interrupted contemptuously. "Not much better'n a rozzer 'imself, that one. Did 'e do yer any good?"

"Well . . . Well, not yet, to be frank."

"Hah! In that case, then, I think I shall trouble yer to be on yer way." Bill drained his tankard, set it by, and rose to his feet again, making meaningful gestures in the direction of the door. "After the bother I've 'ad with the new kid—"

"Bother?" Godwin broke in sharply, also rising.

"Oh, no more'n usual, I suppose," Bill admitted with a dismissive shrug. "But you know 'ow it is right at the beginnin'—gettin' used, and that . . ."

Godwin nodded. He knew only too well, when he

troubled, or cared, to recall his own experience in that area. Which was seldom.

"Don't bother seeing me out," he muttered. "I can find my own way."

He wished with all his heart and soul that that were true.

STILL there was no word from Hamish. Abruptly Godwin grew annoyed. The standardized perfection of his hotel, which was always flawed, got on his nerves. The food it served—so his body reported—was contaminated with artificial preservatives, and was likely to drive him back to Irma, at least, if not clear to Luke, within a matter of days. He felt uncomfortable and edgy, and that dismayingly echoed recollections from the past he had once imagined he was escaping forever.

An uneasy, vague, intransigent suspicion that he had been betrayed began to haunt his dreams. Once it woke him screaming from a dry throat at five A.M.

It was no use. He must go home. The hell with Hamish, who had so far let him down.

As though to make a point, he reclaimed his car from Soho.

Bᴜᴛ gray weather shrouded London; layers of cloud shed their impassive tears into a chill irregular breeze as a succession of low-pressure areas drifted in from the North Atlantic. Godwin, of course, had no need to care about the fact that the street people were being forced to revert to their winter habits even though the summer was barely half spent, dossing down by night under makeshift awnings of tarpaulin stolen from building sites, by day running after passers-by with torn plastic shopping bags over their heads. He woke morning after morning to the sight and sound of surf beating on a Bahamian beach, to the crisp clear air of the Alps, to all the complex shouts and stinks of an Egyptian market, or to wherever else he chose. He feasted daily on turtle soup and venison, on Whitstable natives and Maine lobster with drawn butter, on sweetbreads vol-au-vent and T-bone steak, on hearts of palm and grilled red snapper . . . and then, at first with a sense of defiance as though challenging his owner to compensate him for the disappointment—for the agony—involved in what should have been his latest reward, subsequently with no more than delight and gratitude, on dishes such as he had never dared imagine: strange delectable foods of improbable texture which uttered to the air fragrances no terrestrial kitchen might achieve. All these were washed down with Mumm and Krug and Saint-Émilion and Nuits-Saint-Georges and Tokaji and Mosel and eventually liquors requested at random, many of unlikely colors, glowing and sparkling, oily on the palate or chilling or burning, which combined with the incomprehensible new food so perfectly as to gratify his inmost yearnings and leave him lazily content.

After which, when he stretched out on his enormous bed, a companion would present her(?)self, and there would be further gratification, often as remarkable as the food.

Gradually he came to realize that there was no reason why he should have gone to Bill's to inquire about the fate of Gorse; that there was no more reason why he should concern himself with her than with Patricia, or Elvira, or Kate, or Lucy, or Guinevere, or . . .

The list was far too long for him to review.

And yet something remained: an insoluble residue. He combated it as best he might; it proved resistant.

It was a fact that for the first time ever he had felt impelled to inquire after one of his recruits. It was a fact that, for the first time ever, he had infringed the unspoken courtesies which obtained between . . . well, between himself and those who were like him. (He knew no more precise term.) It was a fact that instead of enjoying rest, refreshment, and reward from his latest payment for services rendered he had—

Stop. Thinking back to that was unbearable, particularly to the (shy away!) timeless time when he had been abandoned.

But . . .

All right! So he had been in a pet! Was the way he had been treated justifiable, even in a pet?

Like a stone in his shoe, that possessed the power to irk. Having nothing to do, nowhere to go, compelled to wait for Hamish's report, he fretted ceaselessly as though he were an oyster doubtful about the advantages of becoming parent to a pearl.

Without having the faintest idea whether one would emerge.

All his sources of gratification wore away. Daily he inspected the street through rain-washed windows smeared with bird shit, expecting the blond woman to be there. At first he could turn away from frustration when she was not and seek solace in one of the strange, even weird, liquors and drugs which now were being furnished to him . . . and which, on the unconscious level, he was beginning to understand. One mealtime he set a forkful of food to his mouth just long enough to taste, and withdrew it, exclaiming to the air, "I know how that was done!"

It was extraordinarily delicious. It drew on a cuisine he had never imagined. It had been—he was instinctively certain—dipped in liquid nitrogen before cooking. As if to mark some sort of achievement in his life, the partner who came to him that night extorted amazing pleasure from his body.

Yet in the morning when he woke to carnival in Bahia his mouth was full of the taste of ashes. He was reminded of the hangovers he had once endured.

And felt cheated. It should have been part of the bargain that there would be no more.

He found himself beginning to wish he had a copy of his contract, well though he knew it could never have been written down.

THE phone rang. Weary of his outlook on the Piazza San Marco, Godwin reached for it, thankful for the least distraction.

It said, "Hamish. Meet me at Whitestone Pond."

"You found out who she—" Godwin began eagerly, but the line went dead. For a moment he was annoyed; then he began hastily to dress.

Lately he had not used the car, thinking it too conspicuous, but now he was in too great a hurry to consider the hell of public transport, the agonies of delay, the overcrowding and constant risk of breakdown. Ignoring speed limits whenever traffic allowed—and that meant most of the way, for although, as he realized with surprise, this was a Sunday morning, there were very few people out and about except the omnipresent trios of police, two men and a woman, charged with a different kind of duty than arresting drivers for speeding—he reached his destination in less than twenty minutes.

Hamish was waiting for him on a corner where in the old days there had always been numerous speakers on Sunday morning, advocating political, social, or religious causes, who always attracted at least a dozen vaguely interested listeners. Today there were none, and the fact that the sky was once more gray and overcast did not suffice to explain the whole reason. But that was no concern of Godwin's, or Hamish's.

Linking arms affectionately and leading the way toward the pub a few hundred yards away, Jack Straw's Castle with its improbable crenellations, the detective said with warm enthusiasm, "My dear God, I'm indescribably obliged to you! What a fascinating challenge you offered! I've quite neglected my tame discs since I last saw you. Every moment of my time has been devoted to unraveling your little mystery."

"Have you found her?"

"Found? If you mean have I made face-to-face contact with the lady—scarcely, old man! But I know who she must be, and I can tell you where to look for her yourself."

He paused, relishing the recollection of his achievement—and it was one, as Godwin readily conceded; perhaps nobody else in the world could proceed to a sure conclusion on such flimsy evidence. That, though, was what Hamish had struck his bargain for, so it was not he who deserved praise for his success.

"Come on!"—impatiently. "Out with it!"

He unlinked his arm, for the few passers-by, bound like themselves for the pub as opening time approached, were giving them suspicious and hostile looks.

"Very well," Hamish sighed, glancing around to make sure they were not overheard. But they had passed the pond itself, a shallow artificial bowl where two or three bare-legged children were wading in pursuit of toy yachts under the bored supervision of parents or nannies, and the vacant near-countryside of Hampstead Heath stretched away on either hand.

"Her name is Barbara Tupper, alias Simpkins. Age going on fifty, five feet five, slim build, naturally fair hair worn long, divorced, one child *not* by her ex-husband . . ."

In a monotonous professional drone he reeled off item after item that he had learned about her, and with every phrase Godwin's heart sank more.

"I think you know her," Hamish said suddenly, breaking off and staring keenly at him.

"Yes."

Who, after all, was more likely to be on Gorse's trail than her mother?

"How?"

* * *

But there was no chance for Godwin to answer, to explain that in fact he didn't know her, had only recognized that she must be someone he had heard of.

Not waiting for a reply, Hamish spun on his heel, almost tripping over his own feet in his hurry, and strode back the way they had come. A few incurious strollers noticed but paid no attention.

Godwin halted, staring. He thought of calling out, but it seemed pointless. Hamish had always been a strange and unpredictable person; perhaps he had been struck by a crucial idea which he felt he must act on instantly. One riddle having been solved, there must be another, or he would grow bored with his mere existence, as witness the lengths he went to to invent problems for himself.

When he had gone twenty or thirty paces, though, he looked distractedly from side to side as though intending to cross the road from the pond side to the East Heath, and wanting to check for oncoming traffic. There was some—a couple of motorbikes roaring up from the direction of the Bull and Bush and a group of three cars approaching more slowly from Central Hampstead.

Instead of waiting, he disregarded their presence and walked into the middle of the road, where he began to twitch and jerk and fidget and mouth nonsense, his eyeballs rolling upward in their sockets. Like a marionette controlled by a crazy puppet-master he shook and swayed and jumped up and down and beat his face with his fists until blood began to run from one corner of his mouth, after which he raised his arms higher and started to rip his hair out by handfuls. All the time his lips were moving in soundless curses. Shortly he wet himself; by then, most of his hair was gone, leaving huge raw patches on his scalp, and he turned to clawing at his forehead first, then his eyes.

Before anybody reached him among the few onlookers who were not too frightened to interfere, he had gouged both eyeballs out and with horrific and appalling strength he had torn open the sides of his throat so that his Adam's apple fell forward in a gush of blood and he tumbled to the roadway and was dead.

Godwin could do nothing to help. He stood so completely paralyzed by the pangs of punishment that he could not even shut his eyes and escape the sight of what was happening.

Police appeared from everywhere, at least twenty of them, some running up the steep slopes of the Heath, some emerging from dark green hedges behind the pond, some seeming to materialize from thin air. Godwin still stood helpless. He was not the only person, though, who to outward view had simply been transfixed by shock. Half a dozen mostly elderly folk nearby were crying and having to lean on each other for support, while the children who had been playing in the pond were being whisked away, screaming.

That was what had been most horrible of all: the fact that Hamish had not uttered a sound while he was destroying himself.

Or, to put it another way: being whipped to death.

At long, long last Godwin was able to move stiltedly away and return to his car. Carefully, slowly, thinking about every single movement, he drove home, half certain of what he was going to find when he got there, and likewise half eager and half terrified.

As he approached his home street he thought his sight was being blurred by tears, but it was rain once more; people were ducking into shelter to avoid it, a mere drizzle thus far but portending heavier downpours later on. By the time he left the car in the garage and made for home it was coming down in steady rodlike streaks, warm but harsh.

And there, standing in the same porchway on the other side of the road, was the woman. He had somehow known (but if she had not been there he would have forgotten his premonition—of course, and as usual) and was anyhow prepared.

She was wearing old jeans and a grubby brown jacket and a plastic snood that failed to cover her hair. Her face was *the* face: the one which had haunted too many of his dreams since he won his George Medal. Until this moment, he had been able to forget in his waking hours just how many such there had been. It was aged to correspond with what Hamish had told him.

But nothing fitted! Nothing, *nothing*! He could not have gone back to a past reality! If she was fifty now, she could not have been ten during the Blitz!

Poised to enter his home, he checked. She was approaching, glancing up at the rain much as Hamish had glanced left and right as though to avoid oncoming vehicles—*stop it*! She was proffering something for him to look at, and waving. He waited under the porch of his home with a sense of foreboding. The downpour redoubled just as she arrived on his side of the road, soaking her from head to foot. But she paid no heed. She flourished before him a scrap of newspaper in a transparent plastic envelope.

And said something, drowned out as a boy on a noisy motorbike roared along the street, attracting all the attention of all the kids who had been, as usual, turned out of their houses to fend for themselves, to go to school or not as they chose, their parents having given up caring.

"What?"

"I said"—shouting now—"I want to know who the hell you think you are!"

"Why?"

"You can't be *him*! You can't!" She was staring at him with huge sad eyes, rain dripping from the rat-tails of her blond locks. "But you look so like—! And where the hell is my daughter?"

She clutched his arm; he shook her off, turning away. "I think you must be out of your mind—*madam*!" he said cuttingly, and resolved that if she persisted, he would invoke the flex. Probably he should already have done so.

"Explain this, then!" she shouted, thrusting the plastic-clad press cutting under his nose. "Go on! Explain!"

"Get lost, you maniac!" Godwin barked. And had to dodge, at risk of losing his footing on the worn steps, as she shot her right arm out toward him. But she was not intending to hit him, only to catch hold and make him look at what she was clutching.

"It's your face!" she cried. "And it's impossible—it can't be true! But—oh, damn you, why can't you understand? It is your face!"

All of a sudden, despite the rain smears on the clear plastic, Godwin recognized a pattern on the paper: to the left, a column of text, to the right, a series of four photographs, a headline spanning both.

And the world seemed to come to a petrified halt.

At long last he said, hearing his voice gravelly and rough, "Where did you get that?"

"I've kept it all my life. Do you recognize it?"

"You think"—he was calming now—"one of those photos is of me?"

"No, of course not. It's of somebody exactly like you called Flight Lieutenant Ransome who rescued me from my parents' home when a flying bomb landed on it in 1944. But I've not only carried this with me ever since. I've carried the clearest possible memory of the face of the man who rescued me. I've been in love with it—not with him, with *it*. I can scarcely bear to look at you because you wear the face I remember. But I must. I have to, because so far as I can find out you were the last person to see my daughter alive."

She dropped her hands to her sides and stood before him, a foot lower on the steps of the house, with rain pelting down on her head, like a penitent at the shrine of some strict but not unkindly water god.

"Alive?" Godwin said after a while.

"They think she must either have been murdered and very well hidden, or kidnapped out of the country. There's a big demand for European girls in the Arab

countries, and—so they tell me—the wealthy men out
there are now too sophisticated to worry about whether
or not they're virgins. Just so long as they're good at
what becomes their job . . . But I know Dora. I know
she's never been a person to obey—me, or anybody. So
I think it's far more likely that she's dead."

There was a dead pause, during which the noise of
the motorbike finally faded into silence and Godwin
compared—point for point—these features with his
recollection of the little girl he had known as Greer.

He had not been mistaken. Barring the effects of age,
the correspondence was flawless.

All at once an indescribable hunger filled him: a
hunger for knowledge. How was this possible? Why?
How could that press cutting match the one he owned
so closely? How could this woman have recognized his
face when it didn't belong to any Flight Lieutenant
Ransome . . . ?

Or did it?

The notion that his very face might have been stolen
was so horrifying that it tipped the balance, persuaded
him to do something he had never dreamed of doing
before. But he needed information as badly as though
he were starved in some manner abstract yet essential—as though there could be a vitamin deficiency of
the mind.

He had believed until now that he knew who he was.
He had believed he knew who others thought he was.
On the instant all these comfortable assumptions had
been wiped away.

He said gruffly, "No, Barbara. Your daughter isn't
dead."

"You know who I am?" She flinched away as though
she had been struck.

"Probably not. I'm damned sure I don't know who I
am. But you'd better come inside out of the rain."

BECAUSE he could have used the flex and had chosen not to, a delicious feeling of defiance pervaded Godwin now, growing fiercer with every tread of the staircase. He was almost giddy by the time he opened the door of his room and recklessly activated it, making a random choice and hitting on Dirk van Beelden's place. She followed him across the threshold into a huge apartment paneled with sleek polished woods and hung with colorful batik work, and gasped as she realized that from gray and rain-swept London she could look out on the brilliant sunshine of a Balinese village. The air was full of steamy tropical scents. A gamelan orchestra was rehearsing, getting the melody wrong, and repeatedly breaking into laughter.

A parrot flew squawking out of a nearby treetop and made her jump.

Pleased with her reaction, Godwin signaled open the door of a wardrobe to reveal rows of fluffy terrycloth robes and piles of polychrome towels.

"Here!" he said, seizing one of each and tossing them toward her. "Dry off—you must be even worse soaked than I am."

She caught them neatly in midair and stood for a long second gazing at him while he peeled off his jacket and shirt and took a towel to dry his own hair. Then she said, "I've been dreaming of this moment for forty years."

"What?" Disconcerted, he blinked at her.

"To be alone in a room with the man of my dreams, ready to undress before him." Her tone was absolutely level, almost chilling in its impersonality. "But you aren't him. You aren't even like him, or anybody I ever met or dreamed of. *How the hell do you account for this?*"

Her voice abruptly took on passion as she flung away the towel and robe and once again extended her scrap of newspaper.

He accepted it and this time actually read it. Under the second of the four pictures on the right, a carefully posed portrait which as she had promised showed the face Godwin wore, the caption identified F/Lt. S. W. Ransome, G.M. The same name appeared in the text at the left, where details of Ransome's heroic action in saving a little girl from a house wrecked by a flying bomb were given in fulsome terms.

Godwin studied it for a while, pondering. Then he handed it back and turned to his memento display, which—alone of the contents of his home—remained unchanged regardless of what else altered. He removed and mutely proffered his medal, and the nearly identical cutting from his pocket.

Mechanically brushing aside her still water-heavy locks, she looked from one copy to the other. She said half hopefully, "Your father . . . ?"

But it was a vain notion. She discarded it instantly, while he was still thinking with vague surprise: yes, of course, I must have had a father, I suppose.

"You had it forged," she challenged now. "You saw the likeness and got a printer to imitate it and substitute your own name—God knows why, since you're much too young for anyone to be taken in . . . Are you really called Godwin Harpinshield?"

"Yes. But I didn't have it faked."

"If you can say that with a straight face you must be out of your mind. I don't know what kind of crazy fantasy you've invented, but I don't want any part of it. I want to get out of here. Right away!"

Godwin sighed and let his towel fall. "You may, of course. If you like. Back to the world where your daughter is given up for dead."

* * *

The gamelan finally got it right and embarked on one of the complex, flowing, half-improvised, half-composed structures of sound which musicologists regard as the next most advanced form after the European symphony. Barbara waited a little before speaking again, seeming to find enjoyment in being distracted by the music.

"You claim to know she isn't," she said finally.

"Yes."

"The police think she must be. They've been hunting her for weeks."

"And?"

"What do you mean?"

"Aren't they saying that the lead which brought them to me was a dead end?" Godwin parodied a grin; what trace of humor there was in it did not reach his eyes.

"They said that about all of them. But there was something odd about the way they acted here—I mean outside, talking to you. I was watching. You noticed me, didn't you?"

"Yes."

"Well . . ." She shrugged. Rain was still trickling out of her hair, tracing down her forehead; with sudden irritation she whipped off her plastic snood and reclaimed the towel. Wiping her face, she concluded, "When I stopped believing them I decided to come back."

"Because you don't want to believe she's dead."

"Of course I don't!"

"Where were you when she disappeared?"

"I was in Hollywood on business, trying to close a deal for a TV series. Dora was safe in school, or should have been. You were seen with her. Didn't you talk to her? Did you just use her and drop her? Or what?"

"I talked a lot to her."

"Where is she, then?"

She had been drying herself one-handed; now she suddenly recollected that that was because her press cutting was in the other hand. Folding it with care, she tucked it into her hip pocket.

"It wouldn't do any good if I told you. Nobody can find her unless she wants to be found. I already explained that."

"Oh, stuff your nonsense! If she's alive, I'll find her. If I have to spend every penny on detectives I'll— What's wrong with *you* all of a sudden?"

For Godwin had turned perfectly pale, shut his eyes, and began to sway back and forth, head spinning with memories of the hideous scene he had witnessed by Whitestone Pond. He fully expected the pangs of punishment to gripe at him, but nothing worse than nausea eventuated; perhaps the owners thought that only a reminder was called for.

He was able after a few seconds to recover his wits and say in a calm voice, "Until today there was a detective who could have found her. But he's dead, and there's no help for it . . . Come on, let's have a drink. I'm going to. I need one."

She still hesitated a moment longer, then yielded and turned to the nearest chair. "All right," she muttered. "You know, sometimes I wish I didn't give a damn for my bloody daughter, but . . . Well, there it is, and I'm stuck with it. What have you got?"

"Anything."

"Then I'll have—I'll have a margarita."

In the cupboard which Godwin opened there were bottles of tequila and triple-sec, fresh limes, chilled glasses resting rim down in a bed of sea-salt. Without a word he proceeded to the mixing.

She said after a little, "Suppose I'd asked for a sazerac. Or a gin sling. Or a planter's punch."

"You'd have got it. Here." He brought her glass.

"It's very good," she said grudgingly, having sipped.

"Thank you." He dropped into a chair facing hers.

"But who the hell are you? And what are you doing living here? I mean, this street is practically a slum, and—hell, I don't know what this place must cost to run, but I never saw anything like it, not even in Beverly Hills! This artificial view of yours—"

"Artificial?"

"Who are you trying to kid? It must be done with—oh, I'm no expert, but . . . Film projectors! Tapes, bottled smells, a computer to run the whole shebang!"

"Go to the window and lean out."

She gazed at him dubiously. Then, with an air of determination, she did exactly that. Leaning over the sill, she bit her lip. Then she stretched as far as she could into the air beyond, as though expecting to find solidity, an end to the illusion. There was none.

"There's a bamboo staircase outside," she said at last.

"You can walk down it if you want. If you're sick of this year's gray cold summer let's go for a swim. This is Dirk van Beelden's place on the north coast of Bali. People here don't mind Europeans swimming nude. It's regarded as a forgivable eccentricity. They do the same themselves, but they prefer fresh water. Some of them are learning a taste for sea bathing, though. At any rate you won't need a costume."

"I . . ." She shook her head dizzily. "Did you put something in my drink?"

"Exactly what always goes into a margarita."

"But—but this whole thing is impossible!"

"I disagree. You see, I'm used to it. As far as I'm concerned, this is simply the place where I live."

"But Bali? In the middle of a dirty London suburb?"

"Or Venice or Paris or Rio or Nassau or wherever takes my fancy. I have friends all round the world."

"It's an illusion," she said positively. "It has to be. For one thing"—with sudden triumph—"Bali's on the opposite side of the Earth. It can't possibly be high noon there when it's daytime here!"

"That's taken care of," Godwin sighed. "Walk down those stairs, you'll meet Dirk and swim from his beach and eat the *rijstaafel* and acquire sunburn, indigestion, and a hangover—if that's what you'd regard as evidence." He spread his hands.

Slowly, as though summoning all her courage, she made for the window again and seemed about to step onto the balcony when another parrot, screaming even louder, shot out of the overhanging tree, and she snatched back her hand with a cry.

Alarmed, it had spattered her forearm with its droppings.

Godwin had to chuckle as he brought a tissue to wipe away the mess, but forbore to comment until, against her will, she yielded and returned to her chair.

Cradling her glass in one upturned hand, she fixed him with steady gray eyes in which he could not help seeing the spirit of the little blond girl he so vividly remembered saving from an impossible doom.

"I won't say I'm starting to believe all this," she said. "But I suspect I may not be believing it because I don't want to . . . Let's get back to basics. Who the hell *are* you? And this time I want a straight answer!"

"Who did you think I was when you first saw me?"

"You know damned well!" she flared. "The exact double of the man who saved my life when I was ten!"

"Is that the only meeting you have to remember him by?"

"What do you mean?"

Godwin drew a deep breath.

"It doesn't say so in that press cutting of yours—so much like mine you think mine is a forgery, which it isn't—but didn't you go to the investiture at Buckingham Palace?"

She nodded warily, as though braced for what might follow.

"At that time when so many people were getting killed, especially RAF officers, it was obvious you might never see him again. You wanted to thank him from the bottom of your heart. You'd have liked to do it in words, probably, but you didn't know enough. So you shocked him, and everybody."

She was sitting rock-still, except for her lips, which framed a single word: "How?"

"You tongue-kissed him."

There was a dead pause. Finally she shook her head and took another gulp from her glass.

"I don't know what kind of confidence trick I'm being set up for, but if you want testimonials from me about your skill as a mind reader, you've got them, and I'd like to buy a share in the act. You could peel the quids off a mark easy as bananas— Say!" She suddenly sat upright. "Is that how you pay for this setup?"

"I don't pay for it."

"Ah, hell. Have it your way," she sighed, slumping back in the chair. "But you're good, I grant you. I don't know where in the world you picked up that little tidbit, but it's quite true. You can't have got it off my granny, because I swear she'd have died rather than mention it. Shocked her to the soles of her black button boots, I did! Respectable little girls of ten weren't supposed to know about that kind of thing. I'm not sure she did, to be honest. Pillar of respectability, she was, and glad of the chance to snatch me away from the wiles of that devil's offspring, her daughter-in-law. I didn't cry when she died a couple of years later, I tell you straight. Even if they did put me in a home . . . But how *did* you find out?" She brightened abruptly. "Oh, of course! I suppose Ransome survived, and let it slip somehow. Is he still alive?"

But that wasn't reasonable; it could be seen running aground in her head, on the reef of Godwin's resemblance to her savior. Not allowing him time to answer, she plunged on. "At any rate I'll take my Bible oath I never mentioned it to Dora."

"I didn't learn about it from her."

"And that's the only answer I'm going to get, hm?" Sour-faced of a sudden, she drained her glass and held it out. "Well, if I don't get any better advantage out of meeting you, I might as well drink your liquor. I couldn't afford stuff like this."

"Wasn't your mother's name Gallon?" Godwin said, taking the glass.

"Oh, my God! Have you been researching me at Somerset House or something? Why? Is all this building up to a ransom demand? I can't pay anything—that TV deal fell through and my agent's a drunken fool and I'm practically broke after spending so much on tracing Dora!"

"I want an answer," Godwin murmured. Seeing that almost all the salt was gone from the rim of her glass, he dropped it in the waste-bucket beneath the bar, where it broke with a bright tinkling noise.

"One glass, one drink?" she exclaimed as he reached for another. "My God, you must be rolling! I think that's all that's keeping me here, wanting to know what kind of a miracle worker you are, stuck in this dingy corner of a boring city. Are you the world's most successful blackmailer or con man or kidnapper? Or did you just inherit thousands of millions of quid and decide to spend them all on yourself and never pay taxes?"

"I never inherited anything," he said, handing her the fresh drink. "I . . ."

He checked. It had been so long since he talked to anyone about himself—so long, indeed, since he thought much about what he had once been—the words he called to mind felt rusty and uncomfortable. Yet there was a pressure in his head compelling him to utter them. He had lived a life of solitude for far too long; contacts with his own kind like Irma or Bill or Luke were at best acquaintanceships, while the meetings and matings he enjoyed (?) beyond his window were scarcely even to be dignified by that term.

Even so, he would not have experienced this urge to talk had his life continued in its normal path. He was used to being punished for errors, like the one he had committed at the Global Hotel discothèque; he could well have become resigned to the loss of one of his rewards, had he been able to look forward to the next with any excitement; he might even have endured the death of Hamish, had it not been due—or presumably due—to his own actions. It had been long since he experienced anger; he had learned to regard it as dangerous, as self-defeating. Good behavior was invariably rewarded, just as bad behavior was. It all felt logical; it all felt *right*.

Or more exactly: it had done . . .

But like the worm i' the apple, doubts were gnawing his mind now. He had boasted of being able to go anywhere he liked; in fact that wasn't so. He could go anywhere he was sure of finding someone like himself— someone of his own kind: Wilf Burgess or Maud McConley or Dirk van Beelden or André Bankowski or whoever. There were places in Japan and Korea and Africa he had never ventured to, where he was not certain of meeting strangers who spoke English. What had felt like ultimate freedom had suddenly, appallingly and incredibly, turned into a set of arbitrary fetters. He was at a loss to know what to make of this novel and intolerable insight.

So he prevaricated as he resumed his chair, gazing at Barbara.

"*Was* your mother's name Gallon?"

"Oh, hell! If you didn't know, why would you ask? Yes, goddammit! Yes! My grandmother hated my mother so much, as soon as she got the chance—as soon as that bloody flying bomb killed her—she had my name changed to hers. To Tupper! And I've always wished I'd found out what the name actually means soon enough to be able to mock her with it on her deathbed!" Venom inflamed her words; she was almost panting. "But I lived up to it!" she concluded, and poured half her new drink down her throat at one go.

"But if she was your father's mother—" Godwin said, briefly puzzled.

"Second marriage" was the sullen reply. "She hated her first husband too—Ernie Gallon. Who got my poor dead father on her unwilling body; whose bad seed, as she called it, led her only son to marry a whore . . . But how the hell else was a woman to make ends meet in a slum district on a war widow's pension?"

"Your father was killed?"

"Like a million others," she said wearily. "But a lot less gloriously. He died in a prisoner-of-war camp. The kids I called brother and sister can't have been his. What a bloody fool my mother was! Bringing extra kids into the world like that!"

She briskened. "But I suppose Dora told you all that about her background. She always does. Calls me filthy names every chance she gets, and to everybody. Damned nearly got herself slung out of that expensive school I sent her to, until I managed to persuade the headmistress to call in a psychiatrist, *very* publicly, and get her interviewed about her fantasies. She was quiet after that . . . But we started out talking about you, remember?"

Behind her brittle smartness was genuine hurt. Godwin finished his own first drink and went to make another; having used only half the salt around it, he retained the same glass, and knew she registered the fact. On her face could be read some such comment as "So the purse isn't bottomless!"

But neither of them mentioned it aloud. Instead he said, somewhat to his own surprise, looking into nowhere, "At twenty I was a hopeless drunk. I was an orphan. I'd never held a job more than a month. I'd been jailed over and over. I still dare not drink anywhere except in this room. Or out there"—waving at the window—"which amounts to the same thing."

She pondered that, seeming to conduct a debate with herself. A few words emerged: "Posthypnotic suggestion? Could be, I suppose . . . but no hypno could explain what I'm going through! Ah, the hell!"

She looked him squarely in the face and her voice rose to a normal level.

"Okay, I'll take your story literally. What happened to—rescue you?"

"I had a chance, and I grabbed it." And he was on the point of explaining what it had been, and how it had all happened, when the words rising in his throat threatened to choke him. He had to say something else instead, and was inspired.

"Same as Gorse did!"

"Same as—?" She looked puzzled for a moment; then light dawned. "Oh! She's decided to adopt that

silly nickname they gave her at school, has she? Well, I've
always known she hates being Dora Simpkins. I must
say I never thought there was much to choose between
Simpkins and Tupper, myself, which is why I've generally stuck to the one I was used to when it came to professional matters . . . *Gorse,* though! It's not what
you'd call an antidote to Simpkins, any more than Dora!"

"She changed both parts. She's called Gorse Plenty
now."

"*What?*" On the verge of taking another swig of her
drink Barbara began to chuckle. "Oh, that's too much!
Why Plenty?"

"She—ah . . . She took advice."

"Did she? Never from me, not since she was about
six! I wish I knew who had that much influence over
her. You?"

Godwin shook his head. "A friend."

"I'd certainly like to meet him. He could give me a
few tips, by the sound of it. Was he the same person
who told you how to grow madly rich?" With one hand
she indicated their surroundings as she poured the rest
of her drink down with the other.

"No," said Godwin stonily.

"Do I get an introduction, since he knows her?"

"No."

"Well, the hell with you, then," she said, putting the
glass aside. "At least I have something to go on. There
can't be more than one person in London—maybe in
the world—called Gorse Plenty. Thanks for the drink.
And the magic. Now let me out."

"I already told you," Godwin said patiently. "There
was a detective who could have found her. He found
out who you were on the slimmest of evidence. That's
how I knew to call you Barbara, even though I would
have automatically called you Greer. But—"

On the verge of rising, she sat back again very
sharply, staring at him.

"What did you say?"

"I said he died today! Messily and horribly and publicly! It's probably going to be in all tomorrow's pa-

pers. No way it could make the TV news tonight. Much too disgusting."

"I'm not talking about that!" she exploded, folding her fingers into fists. "You just mentioned a name!"

"You mean Greer?"

"How did you know?"

There followed a blank pause. At last Godwin said, "But when I rescued you, that's what your mother called you. And people were calling her Mrs. Gallon, and I remember think 'ga-*Greer* ga-*Gallon'*——that's a clumsy name for such a lovely child!"

"But you didn't rescue me!" she almost screamed, leaping to her feet and standing over him with balled fists threatening. "It was someone called Ransome and he must be old by now and you look about thirty-two and I'm fifty next birthday and I want to know how in God's name you trespassed inside my head and found out about Greer Gallon!"

Her composure failed her. A second later, she had to cover her eyes with her palms and was lost in helpless sobbing.

For a while he stared at her in foolish puzzlement; then he remembered his manners and brought her a box of tissues, dropping on one knee beside her chair to proffer them. She gradually grew aware of his presence, and with muttered thanks took the box and blew her nose and dabbed her cheeks dry. Her eyes had reddened with astonishing rapidity.

"I must look like a bloody fool," she forced out. "But I haven't had a decent night's sleep in weeks, and I can't eat properly, and——" She had to blow her nose a second time, and looked around for a wastebasket to dump the used tissues in. He brought her one, not rising to his feet, and settled encouragingly at her side with one elbow on the arm of her chair. He wanted some sort of explanation for what had happened; he wanted clues to her identity in his imaginary world, particularly since no other reward had yielded contact with reality;

but most of all he wanted conversation with someone not party to his secret. That fact amazed him, but it was inescapable.

He wanted someone's opinion of him. An outsider's.

Why he should want it was too difficult a question for him to tackle for the moment. Instead of thinking about it, he said in a coaxing tone, "The last thing I wanted was to make you cry! I'm terribly sorry!"

"You expect me to believe that?"—with a return of her former defiance. "Christ, when you've pushed all my buttons, including one I didn't think anybody knew about—!"

"Tell me about Greer, then," he suggested quickly.

"Oh . . . !" She finished wiping her eyes and cheeks, set the box of tissues aside, leaned back, and reached for her drink again, not looking at him. "Why should you have to ask? You have to know all about Greer Gallon if you know of her existence."

"But I'd like to know how I know about her."

She glanced at him, then away, folding both hands around her glass.

"You sound as though you mean that."

"I do. I swear I do. I have no faintest notion why the name is in my memories. Why you're in my memories. When you obviously can't be."

"But . . ." She thought for a few seconds, her eyes switching to and from his face. "But if you're so incredibly rich—"

"I told you: I don't pay for this!"

"Who does?"

"Nobody!"

"Now that's ridiculous!"

"I don't care what you think about it! I'm telling you!" He had sat back on his heels and was staring fiercely at her, and for a heartbeat their eyes locked. He had to blink first, and she sighed as she looked away.

"Christ, I don't understand you, I swear I don't. Here you are in the most incredible home I ever saw, and you behave like a whining, sniveling victim. Have you heard your voice on tape lately? You sound like someone with a giant grudge against the world!"

"Well, the hell with *you*!" he barked, twisting to his feet in a single smooth motion, thanks to Irma's and Luke's attentions. "Here I'm only trying to persuade you that your daughter got a terrific deal, the same as me, and you start bloody insulting me!"

His recent brief exposure to the possibility of anger had reminded him how dreadfully tempting it was. But he reveled in the sensation for only a moment before repenting, because he far more desired to hear what she could tell him. Contrite, he caught her arm.

"I'm sorry! But your daughter *is okay*, get me? Never mind what you think of me! Most of the time I'm not like this. I just never expected to see a real you."

"And I never expected to meet a real you. So we're even."

"I suppose so."

"Are we? You here, rolling in luxury with knobs and bells on—me down there, struggling to make ends meet from one book to the next, pretending I'm a grand success and making such a good job of it I can con the headmistress of the most expensive school in England into taking on my crazy Dora along with the scions—scionesses?—of the nobility and gentry . . ." She gulped the last of her drink and set the glass carefully on the floor.

Now at last she looked at him squarely, and her face took on the contours of indescribable regret.

"I don't know who the hell I'm talking to, but I don't give a shit. I'm just glad I can talk to you. Because there's something I've wanted to say for years. Years and years. I know only too damned well I am never going to make it as Greer, and it's high time I admitted the fact. To Dora. To myself. You too, because you're here. So if you're still thinking about ransom money, you may go take a running jump and I hope the landing castrates you on barbed wire. You see before you one chrome-plated, copper-bottomed, genuine authenticated failure."

"But according to what Gorse told me——" Godwin began, and heard the girl's grudging compliments in memory.

"Oh, I know, I know!" Barbara interrupted. "Whenever she calls me a whore, she's careful to make it plain that I'm a top-class one, not a streetwalker but a call girl with a phone of her own and a luxury apartment and a maid to trot out the whips and corsets! And the very smartest clientèle—to boot, as it were. To boots and saddles, to whores and away! Get me a Scotch, damn you, and turn off that fucking Cinerama show—sound effects and all!"

He was uncertain whether it would be wise to comply; he compromised, and Bali faded in favor of a gray sky, a London panorama, and ordinary traffic noise. The location, of course, had to be one he knew; he felt Ambrose's would be out of keeping, so he invoked Bill's place, with malice aforethought. It might not come to anything, but on the other hand it might, so . . .

But, for safety's sake, he left the apartment as it was, only cooler.

"Thought so," she said with satisfaction, accepting her refilled glass. "It's all show, isn't it? All illusion! Like my life! Christ, when your own daughter builds a version of you in her head which magnifies all your failings and depreciates all your achievements, it's time to call it quits. Isn't it?"

"Who ought Greer to have been?" Godwin said.

She started. "My God, aren't you the perceptive bastard! You know, I wasted a thousand quid once on a psychiatrist who did me no good at all, and he couldn't have hit me on such a sore spot in a million years! I don't care what you are or who you are, but it's a bloody miracle I can talk the way I'm going to. So long as you listen I can forgive you anything, even stealing my dream and making a forgery out of it!"

"I didn't," Godwin said softly. "But I'm listening anyhow."

"Thank God someone is." She gulped down half the Scotch he had poured her as though it were necessary medicine but foul. "Greer— Oh, shit! You know, you *must* bloody know!"

Godwin considered, comparing his predicament with hers, and reached a conclusion.

"You set out to try and be her and didn't make it. Why?"

"Right in one!" she crowed, and finding he had settled down on the floor beside her again, ruffled his hair with casual fingers. "And for the silliest of all possible reasons . . ."

He waited.

"The first time I was ever taken to the pictures," she resumed finally. "That's when she was born. Because of Greer Garson in *Mrs. Miniver*."

"I saw that!"

She looked down at him curiously. "Mm-hm? At the National Film Theatre? On television?"

"No! I—"

But it was too complex to explain how it all happened. He urged, "Go on!"

"Well, at least if you've seen it you can imagine the impact it made on a susceptible eight-year-old in the middle of the war, when half the street leading to the cinema was roped off because of bomb damage." For a brief while her voice had been slurred owing to the drink she had taken; now it was formal, almost stately, and she negotiated words like "susceptible" without the slightest hint of a *sh*.

"That was when I made up my mind. When I grew up I was going to be a lady, I was going to be beautiful and capable and indestructible. I was going to be someone other than Barbara—I'd already been told by a cruel schoolteacher that my name meant 'wild woman' or 'savage,' and I was afraid of what it would do to me and I began to hate my mother because of it."

Listening, Godwin thought of Ambrose and what delight he would take in such a fulfillment of his declared beliefs.

"And because I didn't know anybody called Greer, the name took on magical associations. If I could be Greer, I could live a calm, beautiful sort of life, and when Hitler started mucking it about, instead of just running to the shelter or the tube and hiding, peeing myself with terror as the bombs rained down, I could send my handsome husband to rescue Allied soldiers and get a medal and maybe a knighthood— Oh, God, do I have to go on?" Her voice altered on the instant and she was sourly resigned. "I buried all those dreams of being a Lady when I was in the home where they sent me after Gran died. I looked at the other kids and I realized: this is where I've been filed—you get me?— in the grand national filing cabinet. I'm down here with the kids who earned more than their mothers off the servicemen during the Blitz, and copped a dose and it wasn't cured before they were sterilized by it. I'm down here with the kids who robbed the corpses they were picking out of the bombed buildings. A wedding ring could be eighteen-carat gold, or even twenty-one! And there were gold fillings in teeth, too . . . I read about the concentration camps in Germany after the war, and I wasn't shocked. I saw just as bad. Knew a boy worked with a gang that had a line into the Fire Service headquarters; every time a raid came on, or a flying bomb or a V-2, they were there, going through the purses, and sometimes the mouths and hands. Had to cut a woman's finger off once, he said, to get an emerald ring, only it turned out to be paste. But he never knocked out teeth, though his mates did. Used to carry a proper dental kit . . .

"Well, that was already post-war. My gran was dead, and you know my mother and brother and sisters— the lot—they all got killed by that V-1. So there I was trying to be Greer. Never made it. Tried. Went on trying. All the smart things, like marrying a 'member of the officer clahss' "—the irony rang in her words like a funeral bell—"and he turned out to be an unmitigated bastard! I met him when I was eighteen and I thought he was wonderful. I'd set out to live down my background, got myself enough of an education and enough of a BBC accent to pass muster, and realized that my looks and my body were what were needed to get me the rest of the way. Only Greer was already dead, and I hadn't noticed. I still thought I stood a chance of turning into her . . ."

She sipped her drink, eyes focused on the past.

"Still, the way that bastard treated me taught me one useful lesson: how to make up to an upper-class twit. One condition of the divorce was that I stop using his name. That suited me *fine*. Before the ink was dry on the decree absolute I was in the only business I felt I could make a fortune out of. Starting with his friends, I built up a very distinguished circle of contacts, including businessmen and bankers and a couple of MPs and some writers and artists, the kind who get patronized by big corporations. I was never actually a prostitute, in spite of what I sometimes say when I'm in a mood to hate myself. I was—oh—the available partner for an important dinner. I was the emergency hostess who could be trusted to sleep with the host afterwards. I was the person with a flat where a secret business meeting could be arranged, and after the deal was concluded I could be relied on to produce suitable entertainment by way of celebration. I was the person who could be asked to show a distinguished foreign diplomat or businessman around London, and keep him company overnight and allow him to think it had been his personal charm which swung the deal, instead of a hundred pounds from an unaudited account at ICI or the Foreign Office. I got very good at the job. I often thought about trying for the stage. I had the makings of an actress. Everybody said so. And the looks.

"And then I did the extremely damn stupidest thing I ever did. I fell in love and wrecked everything. Oh, I don't mean all my friends abandoned me—some did, but several didn't, and if I had the money to throw a party tomorrow I swear some very famous names could be on the guest list. But I couldn't carry on the way I had. Trouble was, the son-of-a-bitch was married and wouldn't divorce his wife. I did everything to force him, up to and including getting pregnant. That's Dora's father I'm talking about, you understand. I gave her his surname instead of mine. I called her Theodora because it meant 'God's gift,' but by then I was beginning to wonder whether God's gift to me hadn't been stupidity. I stopped using the Theo bit almost at once, but Dora was my mother's name, so . . .

"Anyhow, he made a settlement on her and put some money in trust for her at twenty-one, and got a court injunction to stop me bothering him again. So there I was. What the hell could I do?

"One guy who stood by me said I ought to try writing. I thought he was crazy, but when I got desperate I did it, just poured out on paper what was boiling in my head, how much I hated the man who'd betrayed me—nothing of the sort, of course, because it was entirely my fault from start to finish—and he told me it reeked of sentimentality and persuaded me to write a romantic novel. It had just the right touch of authenticity compared with most of its kind, because most women who write that kind of thing have never been in an MP's office at the House, or the MD's office at a world-famous company's headquarters, or whatever. I've been there—the Lord Mayor's banquet, and all the rest . . ."

While she was reciting this account of her life in a voice that came closer and closer to a droning monotone, Godwin mentally checked off the points where it agreed and disagreed with the story Gorse had told him. He concluded that, as he had originally suspected, her version was distorted: partly by LSD and partly by detestation of her mother's background.

Shame. Viewed from another angle, it could have been regarded as romantic.

But then so could his own, and it wasn't. He went on listening.

"But of course you've never heard of me even though I have written a book a year since this new career was wished on me fifteen years ago. I never put my own name on one of them. Not one turned into a best-seller.

Not one sold to films or television, though this time I did really hope— Oh, never mind. They paid for my trip to California, at least. I couldn't have afforded it myself. What I earn pays for a three-room flat, food and drink, and enough clothes for me to dare show my face at my agent's office or Dora's school without being written off as a has-been."

"The school fees?"

"Come out of the money her father settled on her, of course." She drained her glass and set it by. "Got a cigarette?"

He started to offer a cigar, and then recollected himself; despite the view of London, this was an activated version of his home. He looked around, and spotted a polished wooden box with brass hinges. It contained a mixture of Players and Gauloises.

"Oh, very U!" she said mockingly as she took a Players. "Where did you learn your style, you alcoholic orphan?"

"Tried things till I decided what I liked."

For the first time he seemed to have made a genuine impression on her. She studied him narrow-eyed for several seconds before speaking again in a flip and casual tone.

"And I suppose there was no limit to what you were able to try?"

"None that I've yet found."

"Lucky devil, aren't you?"

"No luckier than your daughter. She can have precisely the same. Or whatever else she prefers."

"You keep saying that!" she snapped. "So why don't you take me where she is, show her to me, *prove* it?"

"I can't."

"You keep saying that, too . . ." Sighing, she glanced around the room for the latest of many times. "If it weren't still raining I think I'd get up and go. But it is, isn't it? Or is it just another of your tricks that makes the windows wet?"

He shook his head. "No, that's real. Everything's real. Or as real as anything ever is."

"Hmm! Getting all philosophical now, are we? Well, I don't mind very much. It's seldom enough that I get a taste of high-class living, so I might as well make the most of it."

And she added spitefully, "Especially since Dora isn't likely to ask me to share hers! What the hell *have* you done with her—added her to the string kept by some oil-rich Arab like the ones you had a fight with outside the Global?"

That wasn't worth rebutting. Godwin said, "I suppose Jackson told you about that?"

"Who?"

"The commissionaire I saw you talking to."

"Oh, my! Aren't we grand? To me he was Tim. I didn't think of calling him *Jackson*!"

About to take another drag on her cigarette, she changed her mind and stubbed it.

"Got anything to eat? I'm bloody starving."

"Whatever you like," Godwin murmured, deducing that she was starting to feel drunk-drunk and needed food to settle it.

"Christ, we're back to guessing games. All right, then!" She sat upright, looking into space. "Ah . . . I fancy awabi, and some beer-fed beef, and a dish of mixed vegetables, including plenty of bok choy and bean sprouts, and saké and Kirin beer and banana fritters to wind up with."

"Then we'll go to Della Silveira's in Hawaii. It has a great advantage: it's part of the United States, so they aren't forever asking for your passport. I'll take mine along just in case, but if by some mischance they do want yours, they'll always believe you left it at the hotel. The best hotel to mention is the Kilau Alea."

The sight and sound of London in the rain died. The smells changed, becoming oceanic again like those of Bali, but there was a subtle difference; these were tinged with smoke, car exhausts, and the odors of a densely populated city. Also the cloud patterns in the sky altered, as though a pavement artist very swiftly wiped out old chalk marks and substituted new. Then came the lingering tones of a steel guitar, and everything shifted ever so slightly, suggesting some cosmic removal-man had grown weary when within a millimeter of precision. And there was Honolulu.

"There are active volcanoes here," Godwin said. "I don't call on Della very often nowadays. Too much stink of sulfur. Be better after the next major eruption."

He added, "Take off that jacket, by the way. Nobody will give a damn how you're dressed, but the weather's far too warm for such heavy gear."

Slowly, moving as in a dream, she obeyed. Under the jacket she wore a T-shirt, dingy pink that had once been red, and no bra. Her breasts were remarkably well-shaped. In fact she had an extremely good figure in all respects, one which many women half her age would have envied, and now he had recovered from the original shock of seeing her as a mature woman, Godwin was able to look her over appraisingly and even feel a faint stir of erotic interest, the remote echo of that impact which her ten-year-old self—

No.

No, that was nonsense. There must be another explanation for his imagined acquaintance with her, and he was groping toward it with half his mind. But it was too soon for him to think seriously about the problem.

Nonetheless, as he took her hand and urged her toward the window, from which here also steps led down but this time into a courtyard shaded by reed awnings where half a dozen groups of people sat laughing and eating at small tables, he found himself wondering whether means might be found to persuade the owners . . .

Probably not. There never had been; why should there be now?

But it was a shame, anyway.

W HY, God!" exclaimed the proprietress of the restaurant as she bustled out from her kitchens. She was a
plump, small woman with a marked oriental cast to her
features despite her Portuguese surname; there were
historical reasons for that. "It's been far too long! Were
you waiting for a particularly auspicious day?"

There were likewise historical reasons why she
should put an oriental question in a strong American
accent. But she didn't wait for an answer; she kissed
him smackingly on the cheek and seized Barbara's hand
in both of hers.

"How good that for the first time *ever* God brought a
lady friend! Be seated, please, wherever you like!
What do you care for?"

"Awabi, beer-fed beef, mixed vegetables with plenty
of bok choy and bean sprouts, saké, Kirin beer, and
banana fritters to follow," Godwin said with a malicious
glance at Barbara.

"It shall be done!" Della clapped her hands and
spun around, her broad bottom waggling in a pair of
unsuitable Bermuda shorts cut from something resem-
bling brocade.

A little faintly Barbara said, as she touched their table, then her chair, as though afraid they would prove
insubstantial, "She's the owner?"

"Oh, sure, but this is just a hobby for her. She's one
of the highest-paid astrologers in the world. Very few of
them understand both the European and the oriental
traditions. She does. It was what she wanted, so she
does." Godwin dropped into his own chair and leaned
back, trying not to yawn.

Barbara pondered a while, then posed a question which startled him out of his heat-induced lethargy.

"What does Dora want—I mean Gorse? What has she been offered?"

"Success as a designer" was Godwin's prompt reply.

"I see. I don't suppose she told you she has no talent to speak of? No? Oh, well: that's typical. But in a case like that, is the talent somehow—uh—supplied? And if so, how?"

It wasn't the first time this extraordinary woman had disconcerted him, but this time the shock was more severe. Why not? He knew what Bill had wanted, Irma, Hermann, Luke, and the rest. He knew what Wilf and Della and Maud and André had asked for and got. He knew what Ambrose had desired, and he seemed well pleased . . .

But he had never wondered what would happen if somebody wanted something he or she was unequipped for.

And, hovering on the edge of awareness, here came the implicit question which he dared not face.

I have what I asked for; is it all I was fit for . . . ?

But Barbara had dismissed the point with a shrug, and was looking about her curiously.

"Could we walk out of here and find ourselves in a real street? Could we go down it to a real Hawaiian beach and watch the surfers?"

"Why not?" Godwin answered.

"I see. 'Everything is as real as anything else.'" She fumbled a cigarette from the pocket of her shirt. As she set it to her lips one of Della's prompt waiters arrived bearing their saké and an appetizer of fried seaweed with the compliments of the house. He lit it for her with a flourish and departed smiling.

So she stubbed it out at once and ate the crisp seaweed—correctly, with her fingers. Still glancing around, she pursued, "Those steps we came down."

"What about them?"

"Suppose someone else walked up them. What would they find at the top?"

"Nobody ever does."

"But—"

"Nobody ever does," he repeated firmly. "That's—well, it's built in."

"Built into what? The deal you made?"

"I . . . Yes, I suppose you could say that." Uncomfortably, because he didn't like the tone she used to say "deal."

"Then why isn't immunity from the police asking to see a passport built in, too?"

"Because—"

But he bit the words off short. He thought he understood why. He was ninety percent certain he did. He was also fairly sure he could explain the reason in terms that at least some people—Barbara, for example—could understand. Most wouldn't; they were the exceptions.

If he were to try, though . . .

He remembered Hamish Kemp tearing his body to bloody ruin.

He was therefore infinitely grateful when the waiter returned with their main course and their bottles of Japanese beer.

"You know something?" Barbara said thoughtfully. "I'm taking this experience seriously because—you know why?"

"Yes."

She stared at him, affronted. "Well, then—why?" she snapped.

"Because it's making you drunk."

"How the hell did you know what I was going to say?" Her voice peaked to a volume which attracted the attention of people at other tables; she caught herself and repeated the question in a fierce whisper.

"I didn't," Godwin said after a fractional hesitation. "It just sort of— Well, it came together in my mind." He passed her a pair of chopsticks after removing their paper shroud and, taking another for himself, began to load her bowl with stir-fried beef.

But behind the words there were sudden perceptions

which frightened him. He could visualize her, alone in a bed-sitter after being used to the luxury of a Park Lane apartment, with her baby crying away the small hours. He could almost guess the label on the bottle where she sought relief.

"Oh, the hell. Like to like, I suppose . . ." She dipped her chopsticks in the beef and, having tasted, ate voraciously for the next few minutes, while in the background the sound of traditional Hawaiian music—emanating from a radio next door—gave way to a disco beat and the tones of a DJ with a line in supposed-to-be-amusing local jokes.

For the sake of appearances (and how much of the story of his life was summed up in that phrase, he realized with terrifying abruptness), Godwin dipped into the awabi and vegetables, leaving her the beef, since she so visibly enjoyed it. The respite was welcome, but not indefinite.

With her mouth still full, but setting her chopsticks down, she said, "Not just because it's making me drunk. Because it does this for me. I never had beer-fed beef until I went to California. Some arsehole of a TV producer wanted to impress me and took me to a restaurant where they served beef flown in daily from Kobe. It wasn't half as good as this."

"You wanted to see if my—my illusion could match it?"

"Illusion?" She gave a short harsh laugh. "This beats reality if it is illusion!"

"I don't know the difference," Godwin said, and took a long swig of beer.

"Is that literally true?" she murmured, taking out another cigarette. His exiguous appetite was used up; he leaned back, pushing away his bowl.

"I live the way I live," he said, for want of a better answer. "It's what I chose."

"And what you hoped it would be?"

He stiffened at the gibe; she luckily forbore to follow through her advantage, but reached for the ashtray without looking at him and went on, "Oh, I've seen too damned many rich people without a purpose to think of envying them any more. And the ones who are rich with a purpose are even worse. They're almost always cruel. Even when they think they're being kind, they're bossy, they're patronizing, they do their best to stifle individual enterprise among the people they patronize because they know better. Some of them," she concluded bitterly, "even believe that they know *best*."

Godwin hesitated again before venturing his next comment, but it seemed that he had the measure of this strange woman, and that was reassuring—indeed, comforting. He had, without fully realizing it, been afraid that his long existence as a solitary had deprived him of the ability to assess other human beings. In this one case at least he was doing excellently.

He said, "This sounds as though you're arguing with Gorse."

She started so violently she almost spilled her beer; she had just made certain of the last of the saké.

"You got to know her very well, didn't you?" she snapped.

"No."

"But—oh, hell! Why not?"

"Because she talked more about you than about herself."

Barbara froze for an instant. "Is that true?" she demanded at length.

"Yes."

"How can I be sure?"

This was becoming boring again. Godwin said with what little patience he could still muster, "Just think about why people lie! It always has to do with gain. What could I possibly gain more than what I already have, by lying or any other means?"

She regarded him levelly for a long while, her right hand caressing the tall, cool glass in which a trace of her beer remained. Every pass of her fingers wiped away more condensation, until the surface was clear and running wet.

Finally she said, "Companions in adversity."

And braced herself for his reply, as for a slap in the face.

Instead, he found himself gazing at her foolishly and saying, "What?"

"Marlowe!"

It crossed his mind to say fliply, "Oh, yes! Philip!" He canceled the impulse, and felt furious because she had put him at a loss. Why the hell did this woman, who had on her own admission led a life which climaxed in failure, retain the gift of taking him aback?

He wished he had never seen her. He wished he had never craved a decoration for bravery. He wished he were dead.

Or better: that she were.

AT last she put him out of his misery as she stubbed her cigarette into the cooling pile of uneaten vegetables.

"Let's get back where we came from. If we can."

"You don't want your banana fritters?"

"No."

"As you like, then." He rose and turned back to the stairs.

"Don't you have to—?"

"Pay?" He curled his lip in a sour smile. "I keep telling you, and you don't believe me, do you?"

"Don't people notice?"

"Very probably."

"Then—"

"Then they assume we run a permanent charge account!" he snapped, and even that delay had been too long. For here came bustling Della again, just in time to prevent him having to answer Barbara's half-whispered question:

"Who's 'we'?"

"You leave so soon? But you just got here!"

"Della my love, it's a big wide world and each of us must follow our own destiny."

"True, true!"—with a look of uncharacteristic solemnity. "But is your destiny truly leading you somewhere?"

"I'll be able to answer that when I arrive."

"Oh, wow!" She broke into a peal of laughter. "Aren't you always the one with the sharp answer, God? Oh, yes! Let me kiss you, baby, in case it's so many years again before we meet!"

As she was planting a loud kiss on his cheek Barbara said caustically, "You can't predict when that will be? He tells me you're the best astrologer round here."

Della drew back, something feral coming into her expression as her hands curled into claws. Godwin had a faint recollection of hearing about her background: leader of a murderous interracial street gang when she was thirteen, determined to prove that just because her name was Portuguese she didn't *have* to live out her life at the bottom of the Hawaiian totem pole . . .

It would have been so much more fun to recruit her than bloody Gorse!

But of course he hadn't been given that assignment. He had stuck strictly to his own patch, dutifully, obediently.

Were duty and obedience enough?

He slapped that down, just as Della was getting set to do the same to Barbara, and hastily exclaimed, "Now, ladies!"

"Lady?" Della repeated. "I never knew what it meant till I got old and bitter. And she didn't make it even yet!"

"But he"—from Barbara, with a nod at Godwin—"has a kind of old-fashioned charm, doesn't he? A sort of . . . A sort of *square* charm?"

That was better than tactful. It reduced Della's scowl to a grin in no time at all, and she wound up embracing Barbara and insisting that she come back soon, without this pain-in-the-ass to drag her down. Barbara duly promised.

And whispered behind her hand, "Get me out of here!"

HALF puzzled, yet half relieved, he took leave of Della and they made their way back up the stairs they had descended into her courtyard. He was preparing himself to answer what he thought of as Barbara's unavoidable question—"What's here when you aren't?"—and finding himself ill-equipped when she stepped into the London apartment and glanced apprehensively behind her. The view was still Hawaiian.

"Are we back where we started?" she demanded.

"You mean: will you find London if you go to the street door?"

"Of course that's what I bloody mean!"

"Yes, you will."

"Then I want out!" She snatched up her jacket from the chair where it had been dumped. "I want to go back to a sane, familiar world, and I want to do it *now!*"

"No!" Dismayed, he took a step toward her while a cascade of thought went pelting through his head, powered at the basic level by a single urge: *if I never get to make it with the little girl who sucked my tongue in front of the palace, I should bloody well get to make it with this version!*

At some point it turned, however, into: *I deserve to!*

And that didn't make sense.

He had to flee from that confrontation with himself and found a way in saying, "But why?"

"I told you!"

"You didn't!"

"Oh yes I fucking well did, and you were too thick to notice!"

They were confronting each other like boxers and

they were panting and they held their hands ready to
curl into fists and they were almost dancing on their
toes and the room was superbly—proudly—uncaring so
that they bumped into stools and low tables and the
corners of magazine racks while they circled.

It was funny.

Yes, of course it was. It was like a Laurel and Hardy
film.

He essayed a laugh and it came near to choking him,
but it broke the deadlock. She said, "If you were trying
to make an impression on me, you didn't. But you told
me what you've done and why I have to hate you."

Hate?

Words so redolent of strong feeling were long unfamiliar to Godwin. All such emotions had been left by
the wayside. He said foggily, "I never did anything to
make you hate me."

"But you did." She was drawing on her jacket, having made it to the side of the room nearest the way out.
"That's why I want to get away from here as soon as
possible." Looking about her, she shuddered at the
sight of the splendid furniture, the luxury wall hangings,
the vision of a Pacific summer which remained, clouded
by smoke and mist, beyond the windows.

"Stop talking in riddles!" Godwin raged, catching
her by the arm. Oh, the temptation of anger! It was
coming closer to his inner self with every passing second. To bruise; to beat up; to make bleed . . .

But perhaps that was a sort of insurance for the owners?

The idea was novel, and alarming, but it resonated
with images from Hamish's death. Godwin took a steely
grip on himself and looked at Barbara afresh, as a
woman, a handsome woman, a woman who had had the
persistence—the guts, the bloody-mindedness—to
struggle through a miserable life and somehow, nonetheless, create an identity, derived from nobody but
herself and her own dreams.

Whose dreams, he found he was asking himself, *created me?*

At twenty, what had he known about real life? Had he even believed there was such a thing?

"Let," she said, between clenched teeth.

"Me . . .

"Go!"

And drove his hand which held her arm downward against the thumb so that he exclaimed with pain. Before he recovered she was poised anew to inflict damage, this time with karate blows.

She said, even as he realized he was looking at her unfist weapons, "I had to learn this. Sometimes men who couldn't get it up thought I was to blame."

Use the flex on her! The thought came welling up from his subconscious, labeled URGENT.

He disregarded it because he wanted to know why she was insulting him. He said so.

"Why are you insulting me? Have I tried to rape you?"

She was near the door now, eying it, afraid—visibly afraid—it would not open when she wanted to run through it. For as long as he cared to remember, being aware that something was impossible had been a cure for terror. Accordingly he spoke to set her mind at rest.

"It'll open. When I decide to let it."

And had the inverse effect from what he had intended. Until now she had maintained a mask of remarkable calm. At his words it began to crack.

Edging ever closer to the door, regardless, she said in a thin voice, "Going to make me a prisoner, are you?"

"Of course not! I just want to know—"

"For Chrissakes, what is it *this* time?"

And—what was it?

Godwin stood foolishly comparing possible questions in his mind: "What do you think of me?" "Why are you so frightened of me?" "What have I done to make you so upset?" And the repeated one, "Why are you insulting me?"

She reached the door and set her back to it, breathing hard.

"Let me go," she said. And added in a whisper, "Please."

That catalyzed his confused thoughts. He was able to say, "But why do you want to run away from me?"

"Are you going to let me out?" was her retort.

"But—" He took half a pace toward her, fists clenched, innocent of the least impulse toward violence; this was mere frustration. "But if you go now you may never know where your daughter is!"

It felt like an inspiration. But she shook her head, her face very pale, her voice thin and tense.

"If she's turned into someone like you, I don't want to know about it."

"What the hell do you mean?" he roared.

"What the hell do you think I mean?" She had been fighting tears; now they spilled down her cheeks. "I never thought it was possible, I never dreamed it could be real, but now you've shown me, and like you say, it's no more and no less real than anything else!"

Straightening her back with a kind of pride, drawing herself to attention, though not straying from the door which, from where he stood, framed her as though she were a full-length portrait of herself, she stared at him with blazing eyes.

"You've sold your soul, damn you, and for good measure you've sold my daughter's too!"

A FEW seconds later he heard himself saying feebly, "But it isn't like that. That's not the way of it at all."

Even as he spoke, he was conscious of uncertainty. Over the years since he made his bargain, since he realized what he had actually done with his life, he had had ample time to think and reflect and study. He had no need to earn a living; he was occasionally obliged to invent a new ambition, but that happened seldom, and once conceived, a single ambition often lasted him for several years.

Echoing in the background of his mind, however, was the memory of how he had felt discarded—rejected—abandoned.

Something in the eyes of this woman who (how? *How?*) corresponded to the child he had once rescued was telling him unwelcome news. Somehow—he groped for phrases that might explain her to him—somehow, despite all the suffering and the misjudgments and the privation she had told him about (and how close all that was to, yet how fantastically different from, the version recounted by Gorse!) she *had* found an identity.

Nothing to do with a name; she had borne Gallon and Tupper and Simpkins and stuck to Barbara, the wild woman.

Nothing to do with advantage in the world; she had known misery of the kind he fled from at twenty, ten years later in her life . . . and instead of fleeing from it, built on it.

Something to do, perhaps, with pride?

Do I have pride?

He looked about him—looked anywhere in the grand apartment except at her—and asked, for the first time: "Did I create that? Did I earn it? Did I invent it or conceive it or design it?"

And felt the chilling knowledge overtake him:

Of course not. I simply accepted it when it was given.

Who have I been all these years? And, worse yet: *What have I been?*

HE said at last, from a dry throat with a tongue that felt thicker than normal, "The door's open. Leave if you want to."

She stood there, looking at him; a glint of light shone on her wet cheeks, and almost as though it were independent of her will, her left hand sought the door handle and turned it.

Not all the way, though. She released it with a jerk.

"But before I go," she said in a thin, faraway voice, "you must give me Dora's address. At least!"

At that moment he admired her more than anyone he had ever met, for he had finally reasoned out what she thought was happening to her. She believed herself to be in the jaws of hell. She believed herself to be the victim of a plot by Satan himself. And still she wanted to hear news of the daughter who so grandly mocked and spited her.

"Were you raised as a Catholic?" he grated.

"Oh, sure! Of course I was—eternal fires and the lot! And I thought I'd escaped from all that. I thought I'd been deluded by fairy tales. Until I met you, and now—oh, I take my oath on it—now I believe in the devil again, now I believe in the sale of souls!"

"You see evil in me?" he said, in genuine astonishment.

"See it?" She gave a harsh croaking laugh. "Hear it, smell it, taste it practically! I never met a monster before—I thought I had, but you're real and the rest were just pretend!"

"But *why?*" he barked. And she gave him the unanswerable response.

"Because you don't know what I mean when I tell you what you are!"

After a short eternity he was saying again, with dogged persistence, "But it isn't like that! It *isn't!*"

She had calmed a little; she had regained enough confidence to sidle away from the door, as though she had worked out that someone sold to the forces of evil need not be totally evil, any more than a lion is a predator directly after a filling meal. She drew closer, timorously, and took his hand.

"I want to run and hide," she said. "And—and it wouldn't break my heart if I did lose Dora. I've expected her to cut loose and start her own life for years. I mean, it runs in the family. But there's one thing I can't stand, and that's the way you look. Your face! It's still the face of the man who saved my life, and he was called Ransome, and he must be old or dead by now and I can't *help* thinking you're him!"

She took a deep gasping breath.

"You wear the face of the man I fell in love with when I was ten. I wish it weren't so. I wish I could throw away my memories. But I can't. I'm haunted. Perhaps it's because I know what it is to be haunted that I don't want to rush out and slam the door on somebody who's sold his soul."

Godwin said gratingly, "You wear the face of the girl I fell in love with when she was ten."

Quickly, defensively: "But I—"

"I know, I *know!* You weren't ten when I did what I think I did. When you were ten, it wasn't me who did it. But who remembers properly? Whose past is real and vivid like the present? I remember—not my past—what my past used to be like: permanently blurred, written more in cuts and bruises than any mental record."

Even up to her last remark, Barbara had shown traces of incipient drunkenness in her sibilants, thanks to the beer and saké she had had in Hawaii, on top of the margaritas which had gone before. Now, however, she spoke in the cold analytical tones of a social worker faced with a difficult client.

"And in those days," she inquired, "could you have talked about it like that?"

"No," he said after a momentary hesitation. "No, I couldn't possibly."

"Why not?"

"I didn't . . . " He licked his lips. "I didn't have a vocabulary for it."

She urged—no, coaxed—him to the chair she had formerly sat in, and reversed their rôles, sitting down at his feet and staring at him with fascination. She kept hold of his hand, and he detected that her skin was moist with the cold sweat of fear. Yet she was compelling herself to remain.

"So what the hell is it like?" she said at last, having made herself comfortable. "I mean, you've shown me a bit of what's possible for you. But I want to know—I want to believe—that . . . Oh, *shit!*" She gave her thigh an angry slap. "I want to believe that what you've done to Dora isn't bad!"

"You want to believe I didn't sell her soul?" he gibed.

"Wouldn't anybody want to believe that?"

"Me," he said with a shrug, "I never knew what a soul was or even whether there was such a thing."

"Me neither, after I fought free of the Catholic chains they put my mind in," she said, fishing out a cigarette and finding matches on a nearby table which Godwin was unaware of. The alarming thought crossed his mind that perhaps she knew his home better—already!—than he did.

But after so many hundred versions . . .

Against the impulse he said fiercely, "Well, I tell you one thing straight! I never sold my soul, or hers, or anybody's! I know what goes on, and sometimes I think I'm the only one!"

Very softly, turning so she could lean on his knee and gaze persuasively up toward his face, she said, "Then explain."

* * *

But it had so little to do with words it defied his first attempt . . . although he was at least relieved to find that when he did try he was not instantly afflicted with the pangs of punishment.

Sensing his frustration, she suggested, "Well, how did it start?"

He was on the verge of saying, "I don't recall . . ." —when he realized he did, although indistinctly and as though at a great distance. A shiver ran down his spine. He had a momentary vision of Irma removing other traces of the past from him—from his brain as well as from his body—and was seized by a brief spasm of pure rage. But getting angry was pointless. Remembering, and in detail, and talking about what he remembered: that was urgent.

How could he possibly have wondered whether he had counterparts who also undertook recruiting? How could he have let recollection of his own recruitment slide so far to the edge of awareness that months, maybe years could wear away without him thinking of the subject?

That too got in the way. He said harshly, "There was a woman called Eunice. Lived in St. John's Wood, in a tiny but exquisite house built by some Victorian businessman for his mistress. She painted her face too much because it was the fashion, but her body was incredible. She used to say she'd been a ballerina, but once she admitted she was actually a circus acrobat, and I believed that much more readily. She could twist into positions you wouldn't believe. She was incredibly vain and got her charge from keeping a string of adoring teenage lovers. There must have been dozens of them. I don't know what she saw in me—I mean, the first time we met I was throwing up in the gutter outside a pub— but I was the lucky one. She used to take me to Le Touquet and Deauville, and Cannes in the winter—all the smartest places. And she introduced me to ballet and the theater, good food, good drink when and where it was safe . . . Of course that meant at her place or our friends' places. I wouldn't dare drink so much as a half of bitter anywhere else. Even now." He repressed a shudder, gazing into the past.

"Christ, it was incredible, being exposed to a world like that. I couldn't drive, of course, and I wanted to, so she got me taught by a friend who used to race Alfas. Then I wanted to fly, and she arranged that too—I used to go to Croydon or Stag Lane practically every day, met all the people who were making headlines with speed records and long-distance flights . . . It was marvelous. That's the only word for it: downright bloody *marvelous*."

"And this is the same kind of thing you're doing for Dora?" Barbara said after a pause.

"Well . . . Well, not me, exactly. But all of us."

"It sounds as though the magic can wear thin."

"I was doing fine until you walked into my life!" he snapped.

"My fault now, is it? The hell with that idea!" She had regained her self-confidence completely; it was impossible to see in her the person who had panted in terror before the door, begging him to let her out. "If you're so convinced that what's happened to Dora is the best thing in the world, why are you at such pains to try and convince me? Just because I'm her mother? You don't give the impression of being a family-minded type."

He felt the need to justify himself at all costs. It was true that sometimes he had wondered whether he had made the right decision; however, every time he had come to the conclusion that there had been no better choice. His life would otherwise have been a disaster: the brief and hideous existence of a drunken tramp. He should have been invulnerable to this sort of attack.

But it offended him dreadfully that this woman, who was (*how?*) the counterpart of the little fair girl in the Blitz, should accuse him of evil. How could what he did be evil? Gorse herself—Dora—could have wound up on every possible kind of dope in a year or two, selling her body for no more than the next shot of heroin!

He wanted desperately to say so, yet he was afraid she might close her ears against him. Instead he muttered, "Because you said I sold her soul, and it's *not like that!*"

"For the second time of asking," she countered, "what *is* it like?"

"Mostly it's like—well, more like a rescue operation, you might say . . ."

He made a helpless gesture, groping in the air for words he had never expected to need. The possibility of explaining himself to a stranger had never crossed his mind; it was not specifically forbidden, but without such prompting as she was giving him it would automatically have been dismissed from consciousness. The whole pattern of his existence had for so long been dictated by the need to avoid being noticed.

An argument offered itself. He said, "Well, for Gorse it's like being inducted into a secret society which really does have secrets, and they work."

"I see," she said slowly. She was studying his face intently, seeking clues beyond words from his expression. "But is that—well, is that the truth?"

"Maybe it's part of the truth." A reminiscent smile quirked one corner of his mouth. "Hugo & Diana wouldn't agree."

"Who?"

"Hugo & Diana Peasmarsh. Fashion designer."

"I'm sorry, the name means nothing to me."

"Come to think of it, I'm not surprised. He gets mentioned in the papers now and then, but she has a very exclusive clientèle. Anyhow, for what it's worth, he puts it all down to her just reward for initiative and application. Anybody could get where he is, in her view. There's something unworldly about Hugo & Diana."

"I'm getting a bit confused," Barbara said after a pause. "There are other people who have the kind of—of luxury life you do? And these are the ones you're talking about?"

"That's right. Except that most of them, in fact to my knowledge all of them, don't want to know what's really going on. They prefer to disguise the truth from themselves."

"How?"

"Well . . . Well, Luke Powers, for instance: he thinks all he does is meditate when— Oh, I suppose that's something I ought to warn you about." He looked anywhere but at her; the steady gaze of those penetrating eyes was becoming hard to bear. "You may accidentally run across Gorse and find she doesn't recognize you. Don't worry. It's quite normal."

"Normal, not to recognize your own mother?"

"It's . . . It's the price. We all find a way of being able not to mind." He started to speak more quickly, almost gabbling. "I was trying to tell you. Ambrose, for example: he thinks of it as communion with the infinite. He's a student of the arcane sciences, and of course for him they actually work, because that's what he wanted. You can consult him about any sort of crap—astrology, numerology, whatever—and you'll get a fair and honest answer. Lots of people do. But he's been getting deeper and deeper into black magic recently, and I'm not happy about that. He was a disciple of Aleister Crowley, you see, so his capacity for self-deception is tremendous."

Before Barbara could interrupt, he rushed on. "Irma's pretty much like him. She's a beautician, and she can work what anyone else would think of as miracles with the most unpromising raw material. She's terribly proud of the way the Top People come to her, even if they're only pop groups with a hit single. She thinks it's because she has guidance from the spirit world. So she goes into retreat now and then. Whereas with Hermann—he's a psychiatrist—it's all very scientific. For him it's a question of learning to tap the resources of the collective unconscious; when you get the hang of that, you can do anything. But it doesn't really make any difference, you see, how you think about it." He was halfway to gabbling by now. "Take Wilf Burgess! Did I mention him to you? I think I may have. For him it's all part of the romantic life of a jazzman to go on a blinder occasionally, to get so drunk or stoned that you can't remember what you've been doing when you wake up after three or four days completely out of touch. And of course because he is such a fabulous trumpeter nobody can argue with him. He always has stand-ins, anyhow, to keep the tourists happy. And Bill Harvey—that's Gorse's landlord at the moment—he believes in luck charms, spells and cantrips and amulets. He wins every bet he places. That's his special pleasure, even though he's been banned from every betting shop and racecourse and football pool in the country. He just loves to be right. Doesn't care about the money. Why should he? Like me, he has everything he wants without needing the money to buy it." Godwin finally ran out of breath.

"But you mentioned payment," Barbara pressed.

He surrendered entirely, giving a nod as his shoulders slumped.

"Now and then you—" He hesitated. "You do things you don't know about. I mean, it isn't you who does them. Not very often, mind! Usually it's more often near the beginning, like once or twice a month for two or three days together. Later on it may be only two or three times a year, and just for a day. And of course you get a reward which makes it worthwhile."

"What do you mean, a reward?"

"Well . . . Well, being a success at what you most want to do. The trimmings don't really count, not for most of us, though it is fun to have—oh—a car like mine, or a place like this to live." He waved to indicate the apartment. "But some people, I suspect, didn't know how to get what they wanted until it happened. Maybe this answers your question about Gorse and her lack of talent!" he added with rising enthusiasm. "For instance, I just told you about Hermann. He's right at the top of his tree, and he owes it to . . . Oh, I suppose you'd say a partner. A creature. Nothing like you ever saw in your life. And Irma loves growing things. She has the most extraordinary flowers you can imagine; they walk about by themselves! But all this is . . ."

He checked and swallowed, having decided not to mention Hugo & Diana again.

"All this is *secondary*," he achieved at last. "What really matters is that every time you—you sort of *lend* yourself, you get paid back with a special experience. I can't vouch for the others, but what I always wish for is the chance to remember doing something I can be proud of."

He thought the words fumbling and inaccurate; however, she seemed to perceive their full implications without further ado.

"Like rescuing me," she said.

"Yes. Yes, that's exactly it!" Hastily he made sure she did completely understand. "That's why I didn't forge my newspaper cutting. There's always—not always, but pretty often—something you can keep as a souvenir. That's what I got, that time. That and the medal, of course."

"Possession," she said.

He blinked incomprehension.

"Possession," she said again, and started to stride up and down, giving him an occasional nervous glance. "You must know the term! I never thought I'd literally meet someone who was possessed of the devil, but it all fits, and—you know something? I never met anybody in my life who scared me half as much as you do. Because you're so damnably matter-of-fact about it!"

"Devils have nothing to do with it!" he exploded. But honesty forced him to add, "I suppose at one time that may have been how people regarded it, but— No, it's silly."

"You've told me about all these friends of yours who have what you call wrong ideas about what happens, communing with the infinite and astral planes and the rest of it. What's your view? You must have one!"

He sat statue-still for at least a quarter of a minute while conflicting possibilities churned in his head. It wasn't too late, even now, to use the flex on her, to wipe her memory clean of all save tantalizing glimpses of what she had learned, elusive as the remnants of a dream. He could scarcely believe that he had been able to tell her as much as he had; every passing moment made him more afraid of the pangs of punishment, even perhaps to the ultimate degree inflicted on Hamish.

Paradoxically, though, thinking about Hamish made him more, not less, eager to talk. That death had somehow offended him. And he had already been offended, by the fact that his "proof" of having a right to his George Medal was no proof at all, and even someone as uneducated as Bill Harvey had seen through the pretense. Moreover, recollection of the time when he had been abandoned rankled in his mind. It had been like all his worst nightmares combined, without hope of an ending until it came.

His faith, in short, had been undermined. He had been let down by those in whom he reposed his ultimate trust. He had witnessed an aspect of them which he had never suspected and which he had been led to believe did not exist.

He did not take kindly to being cheated.

Accordingly, heedless of the risk of being punished, he headed for the bar and poured himself a stiff whisky. The effects of what he had drunk with his Hawaiian lunch were wearing off, and he needed Dutch courage.

His back to Barbara, carefully screwing the top back on the bottle, he said, "Pets. That's what we are. Irma and Bill and Luke and Ambrose and Hermann and everybody else I know. Gorse as well, of course."

He turned to face her and said it again: *"Pets!"*

FOR a long moment she stared at him, seeming baffled, and then she gave a harsh laugh.

"Really? And who exactly do you belong to?"

He gave a shrug, returning to his chair. "I just think of them as the owners," he muttered. "I don't know very much about them. You see, you never remember much about the times when—well, when you lend yourself, as I said. Though now and then you wake up with a sort of recorded message in your head: go to such a place, when you get there do this and that. That's how I met Gorse, except that she thought I'd already met her."

"What?"

"It's too bloody complicated to explain!" he snapped. "And it never makes any difference in the long run."

"I see. Part of the deal, isn't that what you'd call it?"

"Yes, I suppose so." He gulped his whisky, welcoming its harsh taste.

"But the police traced you here for me," Barbara said after a brief pause. "And in Hawaii you were worried about my not having a passport. Why isn't immunity from police and officialdom included, too? I asked before and you didn't answer."

"In a way it is," Godwin sighed. "You can always use the flex."

"The—?"

"I don't know why it's called that. I'm not even sure all of us use the same name. It's what I did to Roadstone and his buddies, to make them disremember me. It takes a lot of effort, though. I was too hungry and unwell to work it on you too, or you wouldn't be here."

"I'm thankful for small mercies," she said with a wry smile that came nowhere near her eyes. "But isn't it very difficult in a complex society like ours to keep from attracting attention?"

"It gets worse," he admitted. "But . . . Well, I have the impression the owners don't understand much about people. Oh, they know which of our buttons to press—they give us food and drink and clothes and sex and all the rest. But I don't think they understand about things like laws and taxes and so on—probably not even about money, since it obviously doesn't matter to them. Frankly I don't think they care. At any rate they seem to shy away from people with real responsibilities in the world."

He was enjoying this. He hadn't known how many private thoughts and reflections had accumulated in his mind; he was listening to himself with a kind of astonishment.

"At least I don't know any of—well, the 'owned' who are in positions of actual power. No politicians, no big-company bosses, nobody like that. A doctor, a psychiatrist, a musician, a couple of hoteliers, a beautician, a fashion designer, a professional gambler . . . Me, a gentleman of leisure!" He tossed back the rest of his drink and threw the glass inaccurately at a wastebasket; it failed to break and rolled on the carpet, spilling a last clear trace of its contents.

"What do you think the owners get out of it?"

He spread his hands. "I don't know. Maybe experiences they can't have for themselves? It would fit. I think of them—when I do think of them, which isn't often—as being like invisible angels with a hankering for the fleshpots. 'In heaven is neither marriage nor giving in marriage'—nor getting stoned or drunk or sick from overeating. Like a guy from a big city going hunting, pretending he's a wild barbarian like his ancestors, but knowing there's a hot bath and a change of clothes and a bottle of wine waiting when he gets home."

She nodded thoughtfully, seeming completely caught up in his chain of reasoning.

"You said angels. What about devils, though? I know you said they don't have anything to do with it, but—"

He cut her short.

"Yes, of course you're right. I don't know how long this has been going on—thousands of years? Millions?—but it does fit. I don't know much about that sort of thing, but I did read about that guy you mentioned. Uh—Forst?"

"Faust?"

"I suppose so. Well, he wanted to make wine come out of tables, and get laid by Helen of Troy, and all like that, and it's pretty damn close to the way I live, isn't it?"

"Mm-hm"—with a nod. "So in the old days people would think they'd sold their soul to the powers of darkness, while nowadays they choose some alternative explanation."

"Mostly. I think Ambrose—remember I mentioned him?—I think he'd like to believe he's sold his soul, but he's too commonsensical. Wanting to become the best astrologer in the country, he asked for, and got, a full-scale computer. Souls and computers don't seem to belong together, somehow."

He hesitated, gazing at her curiously.

"You seem to have calmed down, I must say. Do you still think I did that?"

"What?"

"Sold my soul, and Gorse's too. That's what you were telling me a few minutes ago."

"So I was." She had ceased her pacing and was leaning against the bar with one elbow on the counter. "And I was quite right, as you've just demonstrated."

"I didn't—"

"Don't jump down my throat! You said yourself, in the old days that's how people would have thought of it. The fact that the description changes doesn't alter the event. Fire's still fire, even if nowadays it's oxygen and not phlogiston that makes it burn."

He shook his head foggily. "You lost me on that one."

"Never mind." She stood up straight, gazing levelly at him. "This fact stands. It's the worst fate I could possibly wish on anyone, and I would never in a million years wish it on my daughter, much though I sometimes hate her guts. Take me to where she is. Take me to where she can be expected to turn up eventually, if that's the best you can do. I want to have a shot at saving her from your kind of damnation."

Angry, he leaped to his feet. "Stop talking nonsense! I've told you, she's perfectly all right! Or she will be, soon as she gets the hang of what's going on. Then she'll live for much longer than—than you! How old do you think I am? You said thirty-two, and you were wrong."

"You're around seventy, maybe seventy-five. I think seventy-five. You were too young for the First World War, you spent your childhood dreaming of what it would have been like if you'd been a hero of the trenches, you found out when the second one started that you didn't have the makings of a hero because you weren't allowed to. You were too precious, like a pampered Pekingese! You never did a brave thing in your life until today, when you started telling the truth to a stranger. *Well?*"

Glaring, she advanced on him with one finger accusingly upraised. He could only stand agape with disbelief.

"How—*how?*" he forced out at long last.

"Christ, when were Deauville and Le Touquet 'the best places'? I paid attention, which is what makes me a better writer than I can show in those damned romances I have to churn out! I told you I never put my name on any of them, didn't I? But I bet you never read anything I did put my name to!" She was panting with the intensity of her feeling. "It didn't make sense for you to be the age you look. How old, then—as old as Flight Lieutenant Ransome would have to be now?" She clawed the press cutting from her pocket and bran-

dished it before him. "Oh, no—older than that, for
sure! Not flying-bomb time, but Battle of Britain time,
which adds four years. And then older still! I take it I
got you pretty damn square in the belly, *right?*"

"Yes, but . . ." He had to swallow, painfully. "Yes,
but would you deprive Gorse of the chance to look—
not just thirty-two, but nineteen, eighteen, seventeen,
whatever she wants, when she's seventy? Would you deprive her of the care and skill people like Irma and
Luke and Hermann can provide? You don't know these
people! You don't know how marvelous they are when
they have the chance—"

"What chance?" she cut in.

"Well, I mean, obviously they can't—" He was tripping over his tongue. "They can't do what they do for
everybody, just for a small group, but Gorse is in the
group now and—"

"And in hell."

"What do you mean?" he rasped, taking a pace toward her, clenching his fists.

"Why, this is hell, nor are—you—out of it!" she
said, but warily prepared to dodge if he should strike
her.

"If that's a bloody quotation you can stuff it!" he
roared.

"Why? Because it isn't true?" she countered defiantly. "I think it is! What was it like having to be
thirty-two when the war was on, Godwin?" It was the
first time she had addressed him by name. "And having
to invent excuse after excuse for not being the hero you
dreamed of when you were a child? Having to use this
trick you call a flex on all the rozzers who asked for
your identity card, all the redcaps who suspected you of
being a deserter? And what's it been like since, always
running to stay in the same place—staying trendy,
keeping up with the Bill Haley concerts and the Beatles
and the Stones and Siouxsie and the Banshees, the dis-
cos and the casinos and the latest restaurants and the
faddiest clothes and the smartest resorts?"

"But I didn't!" he exploded. "You don't understand how it is!"

"You mean it's all done for you, automatically?"

"Yes, *yes!* Open those wardrobes, I find the right clothes! Every time I lend myself I wake up with directions what to do!"

"You poor devil," she said softly. "You're even worse off than I thought. You don't even get to enjoy what little there is that's fun in this sick world. Do you care about what's happening to other people? Do you care about the beggars and the street sleepers, the kids who've never had a job and never will, the lost and the lonely and the mad?"

"I was one! And I was fucking glad to be shut of it!"

"Yes, that figures," she said musingly. "That must be how they do it. They have to appeal to people who think their lives are such a mess they'd be better off under someone else's control. No wonder there aren't any successful politicians or businessmen in your circle of chums—no writers either, or artists, I'll bet!"

"Wilf Burgess—" Godwin began.

"A musician who prefers to live in the past. Not one who wants to create a future. Second-hand, second-rate, the lot of them. It *is* hell, the sort of life you lead. It must be. With no one better than that bunch to be friends with!"

She realized abruptly that she was still waving the press cutting in the air. Now she checked, and with a grave sense of ritual withdrew it from its protective plastic envelope.

"Now I know for certain," she said, "that whether or not you help me, I must stop at nothing to save my daughter."

"Wait!" he cried as he realized belatedly what she meant to do. It was like having part of his inmost being flayed. But she darted away from him, and theatrically tore the paper across, across again, across again, until it was too small to tear any more. Then she let the fragments flutter to the floor, and stamped on them.

"That's exorcism," she said. "I've rid myself of a demon who has haunted me since I was ten. Now I want to do the same for Dora. Save her from becoming a toy for these superbeings of yours who now and then like to play at being people."

Reflex made him go down on his knees, seizing the scraps of paper and trying to gather them back into a whole. But as he looked at the crumpled bits he abruptly realized he could not see them, for his eyes were overflowing with tears. He was sobbing, with great painful gasps as though he had been expertly punched in the solar plexus.

He let them fall and rose slowly to his feet again.

"Very well," he said. "I'll do as you ask. But I warn you: don't judge by first impressions. The place where Gorse is living isn't like this"—waving around the apartment—"when she's not there. It's more like . . . *this*."

With reckless defiance he deactivated the room.

Torn curtains; the bed with its broken springs; the sink layered with old dirt and grease; the cobwebs dense in every corner; holes in the carpet; the paper hanging down in ragged tongues, the ceiling stained, the paintwork chipped, everything dusty, moldy, foul . . .

She surveyed it calmly, instead of being shocked, and said after a while, "I do feel sorry for you, God. Fifty years in this kind of squalor. It never got this bad for me, even when Dora was a baby."

"But you've still got it wrong!" he raged. "This isn't real—this is cover! This is camouflage! This is in case someone walks in when I'm not here!"

She looked him straight in the face and shook her head.

"No, this is real. It's the rest which isn't."

She walked to the door and it opened for her. From below came the inevitable sound of the landlady's TV. There were the stairs down to the hall. There was the front door. Beyond was the dingy, rain-swept street.

Confused, he could do nothing but follow her.

IT was with a kind of savage pleasure that he seated her in the Urraco at the garage where it awaited him. Something like this—solid, tactile—could not be denied. The thrum of its engine was comforting to his ears. He turned on a loud rock broadcast so as not to hear what his companion had to say, and accelerated fiercely along the empty streets which led toward Bill's house.

The rain had more or less blown over; the beggars and the scrawny children were back, as usual, hurling pleas and curses in equal measure. He ignored them; if they ran into his path he did not slow down, but made them jump to safety.

What bloody business was it of *hers* how he chose to lead his life? He wasn't her son! She was treating him as though— No, more as though he were her husband, or lover, with a share of responsibility for Gorse! It was her choice to be what she was—she was old enough to make up her own mind!

Did I give the kid acid? Did I create the world where it was thought to be smart to fool with the stuff?

So why had he been so open with Barbara? Why in heaven's name had he jeopardized his future for the chance of talking to her openly?

He gave her a sidelong glance, and a shiver ran down his spine.

She was sitting utterly composed, so that almost all the lines had faded from her face. She had zipped her jacket as they left the house, and now its collar was turned up and hid her neck with its betraying traces of age. She had abandoned the plastic snood she had worn when she arrived, and her fair hair hung loose and untidy around her head.

She looked incredibly like the child version of herself whom he remembered. And it dawned on him.

Oh, my God. I'm in love with this bloody woman. I always have been. I never knew it. But there it was waiting for me. Like a trap. I was in love with her even before I knew she existed.

And I don't even like the bitch!

Where had the day gone? It was dark. It was very dark—unseasonably so, as though another storm were brewing. Most of the streetlights were out, but that was usual; a few, chiefly at intersections, still glimmered and gave landmarks for navigation. He was too distracted by his inner thoughts to care particularly. Just so long as the car's headlamps cast their long lances far enough ahead.

A medley of confused resolutions burgeoned in his mind.

Maybe she's right. Maybe I have been living in a dream world. Well, shit—I know I have, so far as most people are concerned. But it was still better than dying in the gutter with a bottle of meths in my hand! Fleas and lice in my clothes, crusting scabs on my body, vomit staining my shirt, and piss and shit drying on my pants!

His nausea grew physical; he had to steer his thoughts away to another subject. Or he tried to. Somehow he kept reverting to the same track, against his will.

Sold my soul? I don't believe in bloody souls! But . . . Oh, maybe she's half right, at that. I have let it all be done for me. I wonder if it's too late to try and be real again.

Images tumbled up from his subconscious, random as a spouting geyser.

Suppose I had been the guy who saved her life. Suppose I'd tracked her down, married her as soon as it was legal—about the age Gorse is now, not quite a child bride. Would that have done anything?

No answer.

Suppose I hadn't come from my kind of background. Suppose at twenty I hadn't already been a drunkard and—

But the ways he had found to get himself the liquor were still too hideous in retrospect. He had to shy away again.

Suppose I'd stuck with Eunice, who recruited me . . . Why is it so long since I thought about her? Is she still around? No reason why she shouldn't be! We go on and on, after all. But I suppose it must be a question of not getting too attached. People like her, like me, are obliged to lead solitary lives. If we had entanglements in the everyday world, we might not answer promptly when we're called.

He realized the other thing he might have said to Barbara about his friends. Not only was no one among them a person of real influence; not a single one had children, either.

A thought so bitter it was funny crossed his mind. He had to stifle a laugh as he swung the car into a long fast curve.

At least we aren't being bred by our owners. They take what mongrels chance throws up.

For what purpose? His answer to Barbara, when she put a similar question, had been half right. He did think of the owners as being from some more refined sphere of existence, where the keen joys of being human were no longer available. From outer space? From some far-distant planet? From the future? There was no point in asking. Ambrose would have said one thing, Luke another, Irma would have spouted garbage about an astral plane . . .

In any case it didn't matter. If they were called, in this age, alien beings, that meant no more than the name given them when they were automatically assumed to be devils.

Called . . .

He wondered briefly whether the image he had of that process matched the way someone like Bill or Wilf thought about it. He had always visualized himself as like a dog: romping on a green hillside, delighted by the smells and the rabbit droppings and the cowpats and the dew, suddenly reminded of duty by a distant whistle.

Called.

He was yawning so hard his eyes were squeezing shut.

EXACTLY at the moment when the horror seized him Barbara reached across to shut off the radio and said, "You didn't tell me Dora had moved out of London!"

What?

Against another and even huger yawn he struggled to make sense of the world. Ahead, curving in the headlamps' beam: not the familiar road to Bill's place, not even a road in that approximate direction, but the wide gray concrete sweep of the Westway, high as a church tower above the ground, almost empty of traffic—as nowadays it always was—and with the inner lane barricaded to await repairs—as it had been for the past two years.

He tried to cry out, but the most he could manage was a whimper. Control of his body had been suddenly stolen from him, not coaxingly and in sleep as always before, but with a direct brusqueness that appalled him. Without warning, bar that need to yawn, he found himself coexistent inside his own head with—

A being?

A personage?

A creature?

The concepts that sprang to mind were *gray, translucent, vast, cool*—as though he had been usurped from the throne of his awareness by something partway between a gigantic slug and a wisp of smoke.

Also there was another overtone: *long*. But at first it made no sense.

He registered that the car was racing faster and faster through the dark. Dimly he heard screams from beside

213

him, from the corner of his eye saw white movements: Barbara's hands as she clawed at his arm, then, finding it more rigid than stone, at the handle of the door. It would not open; this car had safety interlocks preventing doors being opened until the speedometer showed zero miles per hour. All part of human progress.

Half a mile ahead a cluster of rare lights loomed: the next junction, where traffic for the southwest should turn left. There were flashing red lamps and a spotlight played on a Union Jack hanging limp from an improvised pole. It was a fascist checkpoint of the kind he had seen in the East End—how long ago? They would be stopping cars to make sure no coloreds were aboard; if they found any, they would drag them out and beat them up.

"Slow down!" Barbara shrieked. "You crazy fool— you can't crash their barricade!"

It was a source of relief to him that that was all she thought he was doing. But in the same moment the implication of that concept *long* occurred to him, and had he been able he would have slapped his forehead with annoyance at his own stupidity.

Long! Not in space, but in time! Of course! He ought to have worked that out about the owners years ago. From the viewpoint of a dog, say, must not a human seem effectively immortal? Scarcely changing, while his pet progressed from puppyhood to adulthood to old age, and more puppies came on to take their parents' place . . .

And what sensation would be most fascinating to the owner of a human, who stood in the same relationship?

Acts of slow self-destruction, obviously. Drug addiction. Drunkenness. The stress of driving at the limit of one's reflexes, tight-bellied, dry-mouthed, moist-palmed, with a heart going like a crazy hammer. Long hours and late nights in the hive of a great city. Plus acts of strange private significance involving more than one participant. How much would an immortal care about the pleasure of the reproductive act? But he might very well be curious . . .

It all came plain to God in the tick of a clock, and along with it another, yet more terrible understanding.

After any given pet had yielded the full range of sensations of which he or she was capable, there must always remain one other, necessarily fascinating to immortal beings.

Death.

And ideally it should be death in full knowledge of what was being done.

His right foot stamped—no: *was* stamped—so hard on the Urraco's accelerator he felt a tendon tearing.

The car leaped forward like a pouncing lion.

UNTIL it was too late the gang in ambush assumed that like every other vehicle on the road this one would stop beneath the muzzles of their guns, or maybe swing around and head illegally the other way, giving them sport in pursuit.

When it was too late they screamed and tried to scatter, but it plowed among them at a hundred miles an hour, smashing their lamps and flares, felling the flagpost like a giant axe, killing nine in a single scythe-sweep as it twisted broadside and turned their bodies into greasy lubrication for its final skid. Then it rolled and rolled and rolled and came crashing to a halt against the V-shaped point of the dividing barriers where lines of traffic were to separate. And then caught fire.

THERE was no pain, even though his body was crushed and twisted and he knew he could never draw another breath because his lungs were already too full of blood. He had the impression that it was being greedily drawn off—sucked away—by the creature which possessed him.

The flames were like the flames of the Blitz. They showed him Barbara's face, tilted to an impossible angle on her neck but quite unmarked except for a smear of blood at the corner of her mouth. Her expression was flawlessly calm, and all the marks of age had gone from it. She looked so like the ten-year-old he had rescued, he believed she was for a moment and wondered why he could not carry her to safety.

There were noises: shouts, screams, moans, curses, and the roaring of fire.

It didn't matter. The fact that he was dying didn't matter, either. Perhaps Barbara's death mattered, but not to him; why should it? He had seen what he had made of his life, and as a result he despised himself. That was a good enough reason to make an end. In a remote, passionless way he was rather glad.

There was a sort of hesitation. Then he felt the great gray wispy presence slither away from him, leaving behind a sensation as of disappointment and another trace of its presence which was foul as sputum.

Pain happened.

Then finally he was allowed to close his eyes. With the last consciousness remaining to his ruined brain, he wondered what would now become of Gorse.

And did not know whether to pity or envy her, with life before her.

ABOUT THE AUTHOR

John Brunner was born in England in 1934 and
was educated at Cheltenham College. He sold his
first novel in 1951 and has been publishing sf
steadily since then. His books have won him inter-
national acclaim from both mainstream and genre
audiences. *Players at the Game of People* is the
eighth book by Brunner in print with Del Rey
Books. His most famous novel, the classic *Stand On
Zanzibar*, won the Hugo Award for Best Novel in
1969, the British Science Fiction Award, and the
Prix Apollo in France. Mr. Brunner lives in Somerset,
England.